The Golden Sickle

THE GOLDEN SICKLE

A Tale by
DAVIS GRUBB

Illustrations by
LEONARD VOSBURGH

THE WORLD PUBLISHING COMPANY
New York and Cleveland

Published by The World Publishing Company
2231 West 110th Street, Cleveland, Ohio 44102

Published simultaneously in Canada by
Nelson, Foster & Scott Ltd.

First Printing 1968
Copyright © 1968 by Davis Grubb
Illustrations copyright © 1968 by Leonard Vosburgh

Library of Congress Catalog Card Number: 68–28116
Printed in the United States of America

*This tale is for two who will always be
my children—*WEEDA *and his* SUSIE

⌒⊰ I ⊱⌒

THE wind had quickened to a fury that night. It seemed to have bared its white teeth and set them against the old eaves beyond my small window, howling like a live thing wanting in. In my high room in the tavern's attic it was seldom that I fell asleep without the sound of wind in my ears. In summer, before storms, it was a green wind: a gentler sound than this. But this wind was a live thing wanting in and not a friendly thing, it was a wolf wind wanting in, honing to set its white tooth against the host's own hand. I had long learned to hear wind sounds as lullabies in my strange and lonely home. Sometimes the moving air would strike a kind of chord among clapboard and shingle and chimney stone and it was clarion music, calling me to fair ventures beyond the hills. Yet there were times—like this night—when river and hills and world lay in the stricken trance of winter as in glass dreams; times when the wind seemed to flow in panic across the high-pitched roof of the Golden Sickle, chasing itself in full, mad hue and cry. Those were times when I would steal to the eight wrinkled panes of my small lattice window and look to the dread thing that stood yonder at the crossroads by the Grave Creek Bridge. That was indeed the only place I ever found stomach enough to look at it at all. When I passed beneath it on my weekly trips to and from Mister List's store at Elizabethtown I always set my eyes hard upon the yellow, dusty ruts beneath my feet and hurried under. Even then I fancied that somehow it glared down at me as I passed. I would feel the eyes of it following my coattails and the nape of my shaggy neck would shiver beneath the curse of a dead look that almost whispered. From the dooryard of the inn there was a clear view of it there upon its pikestaff by the bridge. And I avoided that view as if I might somehow meet eyes across that distance which would stare me down. Yet at the attic window I felt a kind of safety at seeing the thing. In that high chamber which was my humble home—poor as it was—I felt a kind of heavenly immunity from the curse of Barnaby's empty eyeholes, the twisted leather of his sun-dried sneer, from the almost cocky tilt of his severed head. Perhaps it was the coarse, dark hair that gave it such a chilling sense of livingness. That hair was seldom motionless. The slightest wind would set its thick, unbraided strands astir. And when the river wind stood up and strode the bottomlands, the hair would lay out straight behind as it had doubtless streamed back that night in flight before the posse of Regulators hanged and beheaded Barnaby upon this very spot. In certain of its moods, indeed, the wind seemed to give the head its very tongue: a hanged voice crying its hoarse curse through time and moonshine and frozen river nightfall.

On such a night as this wherein my dark tale begins: this

biting, bitter night of that queer Christmas week I shall never forget, this night when the Acadian priest came creeping up the attic staircase to bring me my long-vanished father's strange and riddlesome gift. Nor was it for a padre that I took him at that first slow and startling appearance. I stared over at him from half sleep, rared up in my corn-shuck pallet and squinting across my ragged quilts as his shadow loomed huge behind him amid the dusty rafters above the stairwell. In his dark, rough, tattooed right hand, in a cracked stoneware saucer, he held a tallow candle while with the other hand he touched his lips, gesturing me to stillness.

"Hush," he whispered. "Not a word, boy, till I come yonder nigh you where we can talk and not be overheard."

"Who are you?" I gasped.

As he crept nearer, the shadow of his thick-cloaked figure spread vast and wallowing across the boards of the vaulted attic ceiling.

"Trust that I'm a friend," he said. "That's enough, at first. We'll pry that apart by bits—like a butternut. It will take some talk to get at the meat of why I'm here."

"But who are you?" I said again, stupidly, but less frightened than at first, for there was a certain honesty about his gruff, swinging speech.

"My name is Jean Tailleferre," he said abruptly. "Now do you know anymore than you did? What matters is not who I am but who *you* are."

He set the dish and candle on a rough ledge of sandstone that jutted from the wide shoulder of the chimney at his left. He stared me a hard, searching stare.

"Who are you, boy?" he said. "For I must be dead certain you are the goal of my quest before much more is said. Who are you, boy?"

"My name is Daniel Cresap."

"Any lad could claim as much. Now what's your age?"

"Twelve."

"That would tally. Tom ran off South in '95."

"Tom. Who's Tom?"

"Good boy. There's no Tom in this. Now your pap he was a stoutish man, you say—with hair the color of torn hemp?"

"How could I know? I was a babe left with strangers."

"Bull's-eye, boy. Besides he was dark as a Gypsy tinker. In '94 you say he ran away?"

"If you're asking after the year my father fled the posse I think it was 1791. It was the same spring they caught Barnaby and hanged him yonder at the bridge."

He had his fists on his hips now and boots planted wide apart and he bent to stare at me more closely in the dusk of the candle's shine. It was that light which caught and kindled in the crusty, glittering crucifix which lay amid its chains in the deeps of his cloak. From his right earlobe hung another smaller cross—of coarser gold, it seemed, and cut in a strange Spanish way, one might guess, for the ear of some rough but Bible-minded seaman. Still it was no priest's hat he wore but the plain, rough tricorn of any traveller on the river road those days.

"Yes," he said. "You favor him smartly. Still I must be sure. Boy, who *was* your father?"

And I took his words for clue enough that my father at last was dead.

"Jim Cresap is—was his name. When did he—?"

"What of your mother?"

"She died when I was born."

"Well, I know that, poor lad. But her name. I must hear that from your lips, d'ye see? I must know this and a handful more to be sure that you are, for fair, my chum Jim's boy. Why did your father run away, Dan?"

"You must know that or you wouldn't ask," I said with a trembling lip. "You know well and good what my father was. It's a sore question to ask a poor orphaned boy."

"Say it to me, Daniel. Your answers are the master's key to matters that may find you a boy who's a good deal more rich than poor."

"He was a river pirate," I half shouted, whereupon he seized my hair in one hand and clapped across my lips rough-skinned fingers that smelled of brandy, brass, and nutmeg. Then he bent his face to mine in the candleshine and the eyes above his jutting, swarthy cheeks were bright with a kind of doggish supplication.

"Hark to me, boy," he whined. "I come to do Jim's boy a kindness. Would you see me have my throat cut for my trouble?"

I shook my head quickly and he took his hand away. He tossed his head in a motion toward the stairwell. Downstairs in the inn's great room could be heard—even above the wind, even at this late, Christian hour—the whine of Jacob Turk's fiddle and the clink of glass and the occasional rough laughter and snatches of song from that night's roistering guests.

"I've come a long way," said the big man. "Wilderness leagues and river miles. And every oarstroke and footstep I've been hounded. They're after me tonight. Hark to that wind out there a-howling. Like dogs. Or devils. Well, maybe that sound is not all wind a-blowing, boy. Maybe there is a devil's voice amongst it. A devil named Elisha!"

He squatted suddenly on an old Connemaugh saltbox I used for a sort of chest.

"But I swore a dying man an oath," he said suddenly.

He stared at me in the weltering light.

"An oath," he said again. "And would you believe me

when I say that I still know the meaning of an oath?"

I nodded.

"Would you lend me further faith when I tell you that I took oaths a good deal earlier than this one? Though not, I'll say, a whit holier. Boy, it was thirty year ago in Bayou Teche parish that I was a priest of God."

I nodded again, staring at him dumb, and after a spell of that he swung his gaze to the candle flame and blinked three times before he went on.

"Yet that's neither the head nor the tail of it," he said. "Long ago I chose to throw my lot among rough, strange chums, Dan'l. Men who could have been a sight better by a little love of God. And who could have been a damn sight worse if it hadn't been for that love of Him I slipped them now and then and again."

He glared at me suddenlike.

"Is it so plaguey hard to believe that even a river pirate has a moment at the end of it when he might want God hard by? There's many a loose nail spills from this world's keg. We can't all die in featherbeds like Baltimore pastors, boy."

He swung his head and worked his jaws in sullen speculation.

"Well, forget all that blither," he said. "It's not why I'm here to preach of that. I come here to bring Jim's boy his legacy."

Now he swung on me in a quick little flush of fury, seizing my right wrist in the tight ring of his grip.

"By Heaven, now, do you *swear* you're my chum Jim's boy?"

When I nodded quickly he dragged my right arm high in the air above my head.

"Then say it after me—clear and slow: 'I swear by the Virgin and the bright Trinity of Heaven that I am Dan'l, son of Cynthia and James Cresap!' "

I began the words in a rush and got on fine till I came to my mother's name. Then it seemed the fresh grief of the news of my father's death—however little I had ever known of him or mattered to him—all of that came crashing in upon me, so to speak, and I fell face down in palms, a-weeping.

"You've had a rough share," I heard him say. "Jim told me all of it. Boy, them tears are better than the oath you swore to mark you as Jim's lad. Jim was all heart underneath, he was. There now. Pull up, lad. 'Tis a rough hard share, I know, but pull up. What do they put you through here?"

"Not much," I snuffled, somewhat abashed. "I'm the tavern boy. I help the slaves. I carry the travellers' boxes and trunks. I tend the stables, pour candles, help in the pantry and such odd jobs."

"And to think that your own pap built this hostel. The coin of chance sure falls queer. Do they pay you?"

I nodded.

"Board and keep?"

"That," I said. "Plus a dollar a month. Spanish."

"Look round at me, boy. How *do* they serve you?"

"Right fair," I said. "Considering all."

"Considering which and what, for example?"

"Well, they hold it against me some that I'm his son."

"For what spoken reason?"

"When the Regulators hanged Barnaby," I said. "When the gang broke up. They claim Pap ran off South with something."

"Hah. And do you put credence in that?"

"I don't know. Mister Turk he harangues me for it when he's in his drink. There must be tolerable cause."

"Does he give a name to what thing it was your pap run off with?"

"Yes."

"What does he call it?"

"The share of all the others."

"The share of what?"

"Of a chest of stuffs. A chest they took off a Spanish gentleman they waylaid downriver."

"Where? Does he say?"

"At a sandbar down yonder below the Devil's Elbow. That's the big bend in the river two mile south of here."

"Does Turk think you know where the treasure might be hid?"

"I'm sure he doesn't," I said. "But he knows Pap knew. And he's kept me here for only that reason—that he figured Pap'd come back someday. That he'd come to fetch me and go dig up the treasure."

"So that you're held a sort of prisoner?"

"Not that you might say. I could have run off. Most boys of my age hereabouts have run off on the river by now."

"Why didn't you, then?"

I felt myself the world's worst namby pamby now because my lip stiffened and trembled again as I spoke. I shrugged and tried a manful smile.

"Because I always allowed Pap *would* come back," I said. "I figured I stood a better chance of finding him again by staying put here at the Golden Sickle."

"Well, he'll not," said the big man, gently. "And you'd best stand up to that fact, Dan'l. Jim's gone beyond the curse or blessing of treasure ary one. If he's in Heaven there's better treasures to be found. And if he's went to the other place it's still better than the red hells he knew here. At least he's beyond the clutches of Elisha!"

The big priest leaned one elbow on his draped knee and set his face close to mine, his eyes black as berry jelly in the candleshine.

"Now then heed me, Dan Cresap, and heed me close. You thought all of old man Turk's rummy treasure talk was so much moonshine. Am I right?"

"I never rightly knew, sir."

"Well, you'll know now. It was gospel true. There *was* a treasure your father stole. And that treasure is laid up somewheres downriver."

He paused then and stared hard at me in that harsh, kind way I had in those few moments come to know and trust. And as he paused the noise of the downstairs revellers seemed to grow still, too, as if all the old house leaned and listened. My new friend set a long finger alongside his cheek.

"Now, I wonder though if I'm not doing the worst harm in the world to my chum Jim's boy—by keeping my chum Jim's promise."

I waited, a little breathless, and watched him reach into the dark deeps of his cloak. And while that hand was thus hidden he reached his right hand quickly to his forehead and made a sign of the cross.

"Still I swore an oath," he said. "I swore to my chum Jim I'd bring you this. And damnation to Elisha."

That was when I first saw the small leather box which was to open so much of terror and wonder to us all. For a moment he held it thus on his knee, hesitating, as if wondering whether or not to put it back and leave me as before. It was a neat, pleasant-looking sort of box, about the size of a country squire's Bible—the kind of small travelling trunk to be found among the kits and wallets in a traveller's saddlebag. It was bound in undressed hide of deer and amid the faun-colored fur shone dully its bands of brass binding and a tiny brass clasp, fast closed with a clot of blood-red sealing wax. Studded in small brass hobs upon the bellied lid of it I could read my father's initials, J.C. The big man stared at me yet, his face split and troubled by a strange smile of perplexion; he clutched the little trunk on his knee till the knuckles shone white in the candleshine.

"Have you any notion, boy," he said, still smiling that queer, divided smile. "Have you the least sensibility of what I've gone through to fetch this box into this small circle of candlelight? Do you know through what nights I've fled and through what days I've hid shivering in thicket and cove to wait for night to come to hide my tracks?"

"Well, I judge if that box holds the clue you say—I wager there'd be those wild after it. Are there such ones tonight who want it?"

He chuckled bitterly, unsmiling.

"There's part of *me* that wants it," he cried in a thick voice sharp enough to carry down to those very ears he had earlier warned me against. "It was not just Elisha's greed after me. There was my own greed after me, too! At least *they* were maybe a half day's march behind me. My own greed was here—"

And he struck his brow with the palm of his hand.

"—That hound behind this brow you see—that greedy pursuer who whispered always in my ear: Let the Devil take all. Seize the clue yourself and dig up the treasure for your own fortune, Jean Tailleferre. There was this devil in my heart kept saying: Keep it all and to hell with your chum Jim's boy! Can't you read it all in these eyes, boy? Eh?"

I was itching to see the box's contents but I could see my friend in such a state as wanted comforting, if only for the sake of lowering his excited, strident voice.

"Well, there's an answer to that," I said. "An answer simple as a chapbook sum."

"Eh?"

"We'll share it. We'll go halves."

"No," he cried and thrusting the box suddenly into my lap he rose abruptly and commenced pacing up and down in the narrow half-moon of the candle's illumination. "No. I'll not!"

"You want all of it, then?"

"I want none of it," he said. "It's blood money like all the rest!"

"Is it the first blood money you've ever handled?" I said, a little impudently.

"No," he cried. "And that's the crux of it. It's got to end somewhere. I want to be shed of it. I want to be quit at last of harking always to the hunter at my heels. Damnation to Elisha!"

"And it's this man Elisha who is hunting you?"

"To hell with Elisha and all his devils! I can always turn and stand to Elisha and win or lose on a wager of who draws first. But there's Someone too quick for me."

"Are there others hunting you?"

He swung his eyes away.

"God is hunting me, boy."

His melancholy gaze fell to the box on my knees and he shook his head.

"Tut, lad," he said with a smile. "I know you couldn't understand that. You're only a cub—too young for such awful moralities."

He came close then and cupped my chin in the ring of his fingers, tilting my puzzled face to his eyes.

"Hark to me, Dan'l," he said in a friendly whisper. "Someday you may look back and understand me. I once made vows I broke. That puts me a good cut below them that never had vows to break. I swore to a priest's way of life. Then I turned and broke every commandment and taught men to break them—men who'd never even read them. Which of us do you reckon He'd sooner pardon? Well, the past is past; that dust has long since settled on the road. But now I want to be shed of all that and make such amends as I can. What's a treasure? I've had treasures. I've risked my neck for treasures and then thrown them away. I've seen men grow rich as emperors only to breathe their last in the gutters of Natchez. Your dad died of fever in the swamps of the Chickasaw Nation, Dan'l. I fed him his last bite of supper with a gold spoon from the pantry of a French king. Do you reckon Jim counts his spoons where he's gone to now? No, boy. I want to be shed of it. What's treasure? I've had treasures. Are you sure *you* want this treasure, boy?"

As he went on with all this talk of judgments and damnations, I felt more and more perplexed. All I could think of just then was opening that box.

"No, that's no fair question, is it now?" he said at last. "Not to a poor lad who's scullery slave in the very house his father built. And I did make Jim that vow. Still, try to understand the mixed brew of my feelings, boy. That box holds a map, I'd say, and that map may lead you to a fortune. And that's as my chum Jim wanted it. Yet he knew well what I know—that it's blood money. And yet—Lord help me, I swore I'd fetch it to you. I swore to him as he lay there in a friendly half-breed injun's hut in the swamps south of Nagidoches and him squeezing my hand and pleading me to hear his last confession and him not even a Catholic. And I done him that last solace—knowing my own life was bloody as his own. Can you conjure up that image in your fancies, Dan'l? Your pap lying there in his last, black sweat and babbling of having shot some Shippingport keelboatman between the shoulder blades on a wild March night below Hurricane Island—and me hearing his confession and offering God's forgiveness when I'd been the very one who'd primed and fetched him the same pistol to finish the poor flatter off! Ain't that a riddle for the Devil himself to ponder? Yet what could I do? He was my chum Jim, d'ye see? Ain't that plain enough reason?"

He paused and halted then and sat again on the saltbox as sudden as he had jumped up from it, and then he sat fingering his chin and staring at the box between my shoes and he licked his lip again before he went on.

"Well, that's off my chest, at least," he said presently, with a heavy sigh. "And I've done my share and kept my vow—this vow, at least, to my chum Jim."

He rose and wiped his palms slowly up and down the tails of his great cloak as if to rid them forever of the feel of something.

"Journey's end," he said, turning his face from the candlelight. "And so I'll go down to my bed, Dan'l boy. Old Jim's poor wandering haunt won't have no cause to trouble my sleep this night. Fetch open your pap's box at your pleasure, boy. And make of its contents what you will. And may the good God guard you on whatever trail it sets your young foot wandering."

"Ain't you curious?" I said with a smile.

He nodded rapidly twice, woodenly, still with his broad back to me, his shoulders squared, his fists clenched beneath his sleeves, his whole attitude one of enforced indifference.

"Still, not all that curious," he said. "These eyes have seen almost everything in this world, boy."

And he moved toward the stairwell.

"Wait," I said and had the sealing wax broken and the box lid open before he had crossed three boards.

As I dumped the contents on the floor he turned and peered through the candlelight. Neither of us exchanged a sound. In a moment he was stooping by my side, both of us staring at what lay there. It was no treasure map at all but the most trifling-seeming pile of rubbish a body could imagine. An old black silver seal ring, a ball of leadsman's twine, and a ripped-out page of Davy Crockett's Almanack for 1792. I had the little page of paper spread on my knee in a twinkling. One side was the month of December with its little suns and moons. The other side was covered with a queer, senseless verse of some sort, neatly written in a crabbed quill's letters of brown logwood ink which was smeared in patches, though not illegible, as if by the sweat of a troubled, careful hand.

"Can you read writing, boy?"

"I can," I said. "Major Henthorn taught me. In some ways now I wish he never had. For I can see all this is some kind of joke. And I reckon the joke's on me."

I sat there all clammed up with the solemecholies while he took the page close to the candle flame to read it more carefully. I picked up the ring and studied it. It was silver, tarnished black as Bible leather, and I rubbed it on my britches till it commenced to shine a little. It was some sort of seal ring and the face on it was a kind of round devil mask with its tongue sticking out and all scowls and meanness and snaky hair. Underneath its chin were two little stars, thus—

And that—except for the useless spool of riverman's string—was all.

"And I was dead certain," said my friend at last. "All the time I was so sure it was Jim's treasure map."

He handed me back the page with its verse.

"Now, boy," he said, after a glance at my crestfallen face. "Don't judge your pap too hard. He was wild and wandering feverish toward his end."

"Did he tell you it was a map?"

"As soon as he come down sick he made the Creole sentry fetch him paper and ink and a goose quill," he said. "So I judged it was to make a map. That was three long hot feverish days before he died. He worked on this all that time—until the last night. The ring—that was from your dad's own middle finger. The box was one he carried in his saddlebag—I don't know what he kept in it. I reckon the ball of twine was just part of his delirium."

I sighed despite myself.

"At least I have his ring," I said. "I'll keep that always in his memory."

I stared at it, trying to whip up some sort of fondness for the ugly thing.

"I reckon," I said presently, "I didn't want that treasure anyways, sir."

My friend chuckled again and mussed my hair in a brisk, kindly gesture.

"There now, little buck," he said. "Don't take it so to heart. You might just count yourself lucky in some ways. You've never seen treasures do to men what I've seen with these two eyes."

He sighed then, too, and sat down suddenly on his salt-box as if the disappointment had perplexed him somewhat, too. He smiled philosophically into the candlelight.

"Still and all," he said directly, "it gives a man a queer sense—to think that he has run the gauntlet of two thousand miles of wilderness and Hell's tarnation just to fetch a boy the joke of a dying man's fancy."

He chewed over that thought for a spell and then shook his head with a scowl.

"No," he said. "I'll not regard it so. It was more than that. It was a pledge to my chum Jim. And I'm glad I was spared to fetch it here."

The wind still drew its long, sad chords of sound along the shingled eaves. Yet then behind it I heard another sound, deep and clear as a drumbeat: the sound of hooves on the river ice.

"Lord," I sighed. "There's travellers. I reckon Mister Turk will be hollering me out of bed in a minute to go down and stable their horses."

"What's that, boy?"

"I said I hear travellers' horses in the dooryard."

I thought for a moment I had angered him, his face took on such a yellowish hue. He went to my little attic window then and stared round at its eight frosted panes. Then he squatted at the sill, breathing and sleeving a clear place in the frosting and put his eye directly to the hole.

"Nothing on the road," he said in a choked, tight voice. "I can't see him, at least."

Then he turned to me again, his face gone sagging and drained to that queer, tallow color.

"Are you sure, boy? Are you sure you heard travellers yonder?"

"Sir, it's my chore to listen for travellers," I said. "And be there at their beck and call."

"Where do you judge they come from?" he said. "From North or from South?"

"Neither," I said. "They rode their horses over from Ohio. The river's frozen from bank to bank. I heard the drum of hooves plain on the ice just now."

"You're sure of that?" he said sharply. "A lot may hang on that."

"Dead sure," said I.

He stooped again at the sill and stared out for a spell more through the clear place in the frosty glass. Wavering upon his high cheeks I could see the ruddy reflection of lanterns swinging down in the yard. Then he made a long, low whistle of dismay and slammed the sill with the heel of his hand.

"Elisha!" he whispered hoarsely.

He stood up unsteadily and for a moment glared into the shadowed rafters. Then in a sudden sweep of stumbling gestures he hurriedly crossed brow, heart, and shoulders in the holy sign and swept the candle from the chimney ledge. He turned to me, his face even more sickly and yellow, his eyes fresh with that hunted melancholy I had seen in them before.

"It's Elisha," he said to me again as if half expecting me to grasp all that meant. "God help me! God help us all!" he whispered. And without another sound he pinched out the candle and was gone down the steep steps before I could utter a word.

I waited long in the dark, I knew at last that Mister
Turk was not going to shout me out of sleep to come
tend to the strangers' mounts or boxes. And yet I felt a new
urgency in the air. I lay listening in the dark and clutching
Pap's box of nonsense under the quilts with me. I had never
heard the house so still. Even the wind seemed hushed and
listening. Nor had the great hounds run baying into the
river road when these newcomers had appeared. The darkness lay breathless as the great frozen river. Gone was the
noise of the merrymakers dancing to Jacob Turk's fiddle.

I could not guess why.

Yet it seemed to me even then that hounds and roisterers
alike had grown still with marvelous suddenness. Perhaps
it was my child's pure fancy that they had been struck
speechless by the sight of something fresh and plainly dreadful in their midst.

✌ 2 ✌

I TRIED to sleep. Yet something abroad that night seemed to forbid sleep. It was not fear, but rather an unaccountable excitement as if new events were afoot in the conduct of my life of which I had not yet got the news. I lay awake thinking about my father. It had stopped snowing but the wind had risen again and moaned afresh among the eaves. And I knew the full moon had come out to light the river valley. Its pale, fresh shine illumined the icy panes of my small window till they glowed like eight hot tiles. The house beneath me lay utterly soundless, not a snore, not a breath, as if all creatures there had fallen into the deep, dumb slumber of winter moles in earth. Again and again, beneath my ragged quilts I felt the six surfaces of the strange furred box that had come into my hands that night from the man named Tailleferre. And it had come from the hands of my father. I thought long about him there that night. I cannot say I grieved him; I had never known him. And yet I felt a cer-

tain deep and sullen disappointment that I had missed
growing up in the company of someone of such fantastic
ingenuity. I knew that of him, at least—that he was a man
with a kind of genius for invention that must have baffled
the ruffians among whom he chose to spend his days. In bewilderment I felt the chest beneath my quilt and thought
of its trifling, petty contents. I could not understand this
small heap of senseless trash coming from the hands of
my father. Such remarkable hands. The same hands that
had built the Golden Sickle. No, it seemed impossible.

In one sense the Golden Sickle was only another simple,
sprawling tavern on the river road—in another it was a
veritable maze of architectural cunning. Major Henthorn,
who—next to Sally Cecil—was my best friend, once said
that the complexity of the inn itself reminded him of
Mister Jefferson's home across the mountains. And yet it
was, sad to say, a wasted complexity—the vast and personal
invention of a man of mischief. Yes, I know. My father was
a river pirate, a smuggler, a slave thief, and a highwayman.
I will not shirk acknowledgment of that legacy. But my
father was some sort of country genius, just the same. I will
try to explain what I mean.

After his mustering out of the Continental Army my
father was out of a job, out of pocket, out of sorts. Like
many, he got no pay for the fighting but was given
instead a fine, vast tract of black river bottomland.
Within a year he had lost all of it (but a widow's
acre or two) in a lawsuit brought by Lawrence Washington. For a year he sat sullen in Wheeling grogshops
and presently, having fallen in with a rascal named
Samuel Mason, went South. No one noticed his disappearance. And no one paid much mind when he came
back rich three years later—the year before my birth—and

built the Golden Sickle. He drew up the plans for the building himself and he slept on those plans every night until it was done. And when it was done he burned them. It was a job for which he had been chief carpenter, mason, bricklayer, and cabinet maker for all the fancy fixtures. When all was finished the slaves who had done the rough labor were sold downriver, so that he alone knew the ins and outs of the place. The Golden Sickle was a fancy enough hostelry for that remote stretch of western Virginia but it would have been an elegant tavern in any county of England. Not that it was parqueted and gilted—that would have offended the local custom. Rather it was complex and Yankeeishly ingenious, like a fine piece of native American cabinetry. All of my father's twisted gifts went into that building. Its walled back garden was wild and fragrant with roses and apple trees and willows and scuppernong vines and the garden pathed and paved with square-sawed flagstones into which was set a great sickle of pale yellow limestone. Its stables were stalled with the best-blooded horses and its wine cellar stocked with the finest Madeiras and Oportos.

But it was the building proper which served my father best. Its hidden passages saved dozens of cutthroats from capture. Its secret rooms had hidden hunted robbers for weeks on end and served as prison for many a stolen slave. From its stony wine cellar wound a tunnel which ran a half mile off from the house, opening into a thicket of concealing willows on the river shore far below. Its thick walls were riddled with secret runways and the fine mahogany panelling hid sliding doors a-plenty into heaven knows what wandering ways. A normal tavern full of such rogues would have been burned to its foundation by the first troop of Regulators that followed a fugitive to its gates. But it was long before anything could be proven. The very complexity of the place seemed beyond the average man's imagination. And when the end did come, the hanging of Barnaby Thorn and my father's flight South seemed to appease the mob's temper.

I grew up in that inn; I was always prowling and poking round. By the time I was six I knew secret places: exits, entrances, sliding panels, hidden cubbies, and shadowy egresses that old Jacob Turk or his poor wife Meg would never know. It was as if I had enough of my father's own mind to sense that a secret panel would be just right in such a place and, searching, I would find that, indeed, it had been. I would guess that most boys like secret places. And so I have often thought what a wonderland that great house would have been to a boy with a kind, loving mother and father. But then what sort of average parents would have built such a place? And for what normal purpose? I used to dream of this now and then but gave it up early. Old Turk and his wife had raised me as a kind of bait for my pap—I learned that early, too. If it hadn't been for Sally Cecil and Major Henthorn I don't know what I'd have done. The Major taught me to read and cipher and Sally was the daughter of Meg Turk's youngest sister who, with her husband, had been murdered by Indians somewhere up Fever River. Sally was my age. And we shared a similarly shaky footing in that strange household. I was really an indentured servant—a slave just as much as old Ben and Martha, except for my skin. And poor little Sally was not much better off. Jacob Turk had no stomach for children of any kind and if it hadn't been for Meg we'd have both been worse hard up than we were.

So I lay there that night fingering the box full of the trinkets of that poor man's last madness. I felt all the great Golden Sickle standing so solid around me and I felt a moment's pride in my pap. Then the wind made a sound like a laugh; a mean little chuckle among the clapboards. And I thought of all my pap's mother wit and cunning withered down to this. I shook the box like a rotten hickory nut and sat up in the single thin ray of cold moonshine. Sleep was beyond me. I flung back the bedclothes and pulled on my britches and blouse. My bare toes curled on the smooth boards of the cold attic floor as I stole to the stairway. Soundlessly I crept down the steps, taking two in one long, slow stride to avoid a board I knew was noisy: it would squawk like a catbird at the slightest pressure. The long white-washed walls of the second-floor hallway stretched to the tiny glitter of a candle in a storm lamp set in the sill of the far north window. I counted my icy footsteps to that familiar door.

"Sally, it's me," I whispered.

"Dan? Come in, come in. You'll catch your death out there!"

It was a tiny room with one high casement window but was cheerful here in winter because there was always a little fire snapping in the grate. That cheery flame had dwindled now to blowing clinkers but the light of the fire still washed the shadows with reds and yellows. Sally sat up in her bed, which was small like the room—not much bigger than a trundle bed but with a spooled head and foot. A fox barked somewhere down amid the cold winter willows. The fireshine mingled with a thin blue shaft of moonlight which poured in from the deepset window. I stole inside and softly shut the door, easing the wood latch noiselessly in place behind me.

"I couldn't sleep a bit neither," she said. "Such comings and goings up and down the hall tonight. Warm your poor feet by the hearth, Dan'l m'love."

But I had things to tell her. As I quickly crossed the bright rag rug to her bedside her face turned, following me. It was a feeling near jealousy how she, who had been blind since infancy, seemed to have special senses in her dark eyes. She had always been dear to me as kin, for we had grown up together close as two spoons in a dish and lonely as wild birds in a winter wood. She was a solemn, strange little girl most of the time: proud of her blindness as if it were itself a special vision and always boasting to me of the hidden worlds that I would never see but which were commonplace to her sight as my dull nose beyond my face. Sometimes she was a caution and a trial—with her omens and visions and such—but she commonly came out right about things she said would come to pass and she was always seeing things beyond the edge of Now that sometimes gave me the shivers. Sally was pretty as the carved face on a peddler's cameo, with skin pale as cold milk, and her blind eyes were the livest-looking eyes in the world: great dark pools they were and lash-fringed like Spanish lace. She always bragged that she'd inherited her fine thin ankles from her poor murdered mother and her fingers that were slim and tranquil in her lap till they came to life at the touch of something and then they'd move swift upon it as the antennae of a moth. She had a head full of old ballets and was always singing herself some dark, sad song of Gypsies and raggle-taggle queens and green-gowned ladies, and sometimes she swore hers was the soul of Scotch Mary Hamilton who was hanged once in an old-time scary song.

Now she tilted her round face to me as I sat on the apostle quilt and pressed the strange box into her hands. For a moment they rested upon it and I watched then as her fingers danced soundlessly up and down over every inch of its surface.

"It's a pretty chest, Dan. But, Lord, it smells of fever. Where'd you get it?"

"A man named Tailleferre fetched it to me tonight."

I watched as she lifted it, shaking it till it rattled like a dicer's cup, then holding the soft deer fur of it to her cheek as if she thought something within might speak like a sea-shell.

. "It's such a pretty box, Dan. Can I feel what's in it?"

"Sure," I said and sat watching her, silent, envious.

She opened the little chest and spilled the trinkets across her lap. She fingered the spool of twine a spell, then the silver ring and the wrinkled yellow page, and then put them all back neat inside and softly shut the lid. Her face fixed on me an instant before she reached up a forefinger and touched my cheek.

"You've been crying," she said. "What's wrong, Dan?"

I turned away from her, shoving my hands in my pockets, my eyes lost in the blowing coals in the grate.

"I wasn't crying."

"Yes you were."

"Well, I only cried a sniffle or two. And it was a good while back."

"No matter. You know I can smell tears like rain a-coming, Dan. What's the matter?"

"The man who brought me this chest tonight—he brought some news, too."

He paused, sensing.

"Who's dead, Dan?"

"My pap. Months ago. Way down in the Chickasaw Nation."

She was still awhile, breathing, and I heard the she fox bark three times more somewhere behind the wind.

"I'm sorry, Dan love," she said and gave my hand a quick squeeze.

"Well, I'm not," I said boldly. "In a lot of good ways I'm glad of it, Sally."

"Why, Dan love?"

"Well, mainly because it makes us real equals now—you and me."

"You mean because I said that about you being better off than me, Dan? You mean because I said you were only half an orphan?"

"Mainly. I've been touchy about that ever since you said it, Sally."

"Ah, I was only teasing, Dan'l."

"Well, it's good just the same. It's good to know you and me are both equalized, so to speak. Sally, you know how kin-close you and me have always been. And then here this last year or two—well, it's been like queer, slow changes setting in to the both of us."

"We're a-growing up, Dan'l love."

I studied that over a spell. And I tell you it didn't make me feel a bit easier. Sally and I had always been like brothers and here of late she had taken on a troubling air—always wanting to touch and calling me "Dan'l m'love" even in front of Major Henthorn and the slaves, who thought it was the biggest joke in the world. We had always had such a good, hard life together, Sally and me, and now it was like something soft and dangerous slowly coming between us.

"Who else died tonight, Dan love?" she whispered.

I looked at her face and it had that queer look that used to make the slaves in the pantry roll their white eyes and turn away and I wondered who it could be because she didn't often miss.

"Just Pap," I said, and she didn't answer that.

"I'll bet your pap was the finest gentleman, Dan'l," she said. "And I'll bet he died like a fine gentleman, too."

"That he did," I cried aloud, striding barefoot to the windowsill and leaning on my knuckles into the window seat. I stared through a fine mist of tears into the lamb's-wool frost on the pane. "He died fighting Delawares," I went on, blathering lies like a drunkard. "And Choctaws and Mingoes, too. There was a pack of them jumped him in the swamps away down yonder. And my pap he was protecting the women and children—"

Lord, I felt such a fool. I shut up directly and bit my lip and cursed my tears and cursed poor Pap and cursed the big man Tailleferre and hoped Sally hadn't heard the little hiccup of a sob I hadn't been able to smother. I gave up then and turned to her in the faint light and let those dark, firelit eyes of hers take their strange, sensing pleasure of me.

"You always know when I'm a-lying."

"No, Dan'l. It may all be gospel true."

"It's not true. You know well and good what my pap was."

"And are you ashamed of that, Dan m'love?"

"No. I'm not. In most ways I'm proud of it. It takes spunk to be a river pirate. More spunk than most of these blatherskite settlers in the bottomlands would ever have. Besides, my pap he fought for the Old Thirteen when many of them was Tories and bobtail turncoats. I'm thinking of old Jacob Turk himself, Sally—your own uncle, though not flesh and blood and no fault of yours that your poor aunt married him. I'm just remembering four years ago this very week when the circuit rider brought the news of Gen'l Washington's death. I mind how I got a stout thrashing for climbing the tavern signpost to drape it in black bunting and for wearing a black ribbon in the buttonhole of my Sunday coat. Pap, he would have mourned. He swore by the old Gen'l. Yes, I'm proud of my pap, Sally

—pirate or no. And if it wasn't for you and Major Henthorn I reckon I'd run off downriver and take a good crack at pirating myself."

"Be damn, you're brave enough for it, Dan'l m'love," she cried softly, her blind eyes glittering with tears of her own.

"I'm not brave," I said with a shrug. "I've got tears on my cheeks right this very minute just pondering over poor Pap."

"I know you do, Dan."

"And I lied brazen to you," I said. "That man Tailleferre that carried me the news of Pap's death—he claimed Pap died raving stark mad. Mad enough to have him fetch me that little fool chest and that handful of no account truck and call it the map to a treasure."

"Treasure? treasure?" she exclaimed. "What treasure, Dan? Oh, I dreamed of a treasure last night!"

So then I told her most of what the big Frenchman had told me. And her face got all pink with excitement and as I went on she slapped her knees with her fists till I felt impatient with the certainty that she saw into some of the business that I hadn't turned up yet.

"It was nothing but a scribble of clishmaclaver on a page torn out of Davy's Almanack," I said forlornly. "And he vowed to the poor soul it was a treasure map and made him swear an oath to fetch it to me through ten thousand miles of Wilderness and injuns and wolves."

"You mean that little piece of paper with the verse written on the back of it?" she said quickly.

"How do you know it's a verse?"

And she kept on about it, pushing me into reading it to her till I gave up and fetched the scrap of nonsense out of the chest again and held it up, squinting to see the writing.

There was a little light from the dying fire and some moon blue in the curtains but it wanted more light, so I fetched a flint from my britches and struck flame to the candle in the little pewter stick that stood on the horsehair trunk by the window, and I crouched down behind Sally's bolster so's the light wouldn't show beneath the door. Major Henthorn had learned me reading better than that plaguety Shaker schoolmaster in Elizabethtown, but the writing was brown as dried blood and smeared from swamp mists, I judged, or maybe from the drops of poor Pap's last sick sweat. So I fetched up my best wits and took my time about it while Sally listened and nodded as I whispered it out slowly, word by careful word:

> Queen of Batavia, helter skelter
> Fled to Madeira's glassy shelter
> Gemini in Heaven point their light
> Heed not wrong but Hew to the Right—

"Hush, Dan."

She had said it suddenly and reached out a hand to feel for my lips. Her face was tilted as if she had heard something and she kept her fingers over my mouth. I figured it was old Jacob Turk who used to thrash me whenever he caught me in Sally's room at night. So I waited a spell without breathing, my hand held ready to douse the candle flame and duck under the bed.

"Is it your uncle?" I said directly.

"No," she said.

"Are you sure?"

"He's dead drunk sleeping and snoring like a mud dauber."

"What is it, Sally?"

"I can't tell. Hush awhile, Dan."

I strained my poor ears to hear what she might be hearing beneath the cold sough of wind that shouldered against the house.

"It's stopped now," she said then.

"Are you sure you heard it?"

"I heard it plain. Yonder. Way down the hall. The queerest kind of sound."

"What kind?"

" 'Twas the noise of dragging," she said.

"There was travellers come across the river tonight."

"It's let up now," she said.

"Maybe it's one of them fetching in a trunk that was missed."

"That was a dragging out," she said. "Not a dragging in."

"Maybe the slaves fetched in the wrong box."

"It was no trunk, I tell you."

"What then?"

"It sounded soft," she said.

"Like a bail? Or a saddlebag?"

"Like a side of beef," she whispered. "Or a great, cold carcass of mutton."

"Christmas is a day off. It was likely your uncle fetching in some provision."

"I tell you he's rummed under since the clock struck midnight."

"There's an old loose shutter downstairs at the north window of the pantry. Sometimes it drags and cries when the wind is up."

But she shook her head and opened her eyes and turned her ear to me again.

"Never mind it," she said. "It's let up now, whatever. Go on, Dan m'love. Read on."

"What's the good, Sally? It's just poor Pap's babbling verse."

"Please, Dan. Read on!"

So I followed my finger back to the place again and held the blotted, dim page down into the steady circle of light. I cleared my throat and went whispering on—

> Heed not wrong but Hew to the Right
> Mark not the Phase which Only seems
> But under the sway of Pollux beams:
> Mexican cob and Spaniard's doubloon
> Lie hidden—

Once more I stopped. Hadn't I heard it myself this time? —The faintest susurration of a long and scuffling shuffle somewhere beyond the very continent's rim of sound?—A sound as faint as the wings of an owl.

I glanced swiftly to Sally's face to confirm it. But she seemed so intent on my reading that I was sure she had heard nothing. I quickly finished—

> Lie hidden beneath the Full of the Moon
> There is no scoundrel still alive
> Knows these lie where the Hand is at Five.

I shrugged and felt a bigger fool than ever and cursed my pap again, sick or well, dead or alive, for what seemed to me the worst and meanest kind of joke in the world.

"And that's all," I said, having wound up the poem, and I stuffed the fool paper back in the box and snapped the lid again. "Maybe Pap was crazy with the fever and then again maybe he was just making me the butt of some ornery joke. Maybe he—"

Sally had made no sound; she had not moved. I glanced quickly at her face. Her eyes were shut, the lids trembling and her mouth gone thin and the color all drained from her

cheeks. She was trembling till I heard the ropes squeak under the featherbed.

"Dan, douse the candle!"

I did it and felt the hot tallow on my fingers where I'd
pinched the flame in two and the shadows leaped back
again like dusky curtains falling round. Sally's bed was too
low to crawl under so I lay low beyond it, on the side toward the window across whose sill the moonlight flowed
like smoke. The fire in the grate was almost gone—just
enough banked orange coals to stain the shadows with
faint blushes. And we both heard it now. It was plain, beyond the door—the dragging past of something down the
hall, and the low contentious mutter of men's voices.

"Crikey, but this is a heavy one. Give us a hand here,
Prettijohn."

"Never mind that, Mister Blue. Hold on a spell. This'll
wait."

"What's up. Why are you at the door there?"

"I allowed I seen a light beneath the crack."

"That's the gal's room, Prettijohn. Don't bother with
her. He wouldn't have hid it with a child."

"Well then, where?"

"Dog if I know. Elisha thinks he give it to old Turk. And
maybe old Turk hid it somewheres. Maybe in the attic. Elisha's hunting around up there now. Meanwhile, let's get
on with this. It's a leaky business."

"No fear. I wropped burlap round it good."

"Well, I still want to get shut of it. What are you about?"

"I'm just going to give a look round in the gal's room to
be sure. It'd be a feather in both our caps if I was to walk in
there and find it lying somewheres in plain sight. Elisha,
he'd like that."

Sally commenced snoring lightly and so real I was proud

enough of her to holler but I held my breath and listened while a hand softly drew the latch string. Through the space between bed and floor I could see the door swing slowly open.

"It was the light in the fire yonder that you seen," whispered the man named Blue.

But Prettijohn stole into the room—I could see the big hobbed boots of him like the ones keelboatmen wore and I could even smell the rank air about him of sweat and Fundador brandy and the cheap hot German sausage he had eaten. He came stealthy-toed to the edge of Sally's bed and I judged he was bending to look at the face of her pressed tight and feigning sleep amid the feather bolster.

"She's a pretty little lambkin," Prettijohn said.

"Well, we're here to deal with sheep, not lambs," said Blue. "Come on. I want to get this other business over with, Prettijohn. It's an ugly fancy of Elisha's and not to my liking. Let's get on with it."

But Prettijohn tarried longer, pleasuring himself at the sight of Sally there, I reckoned, and I thought of the hot poker in the grate: it would be my only weapon to protect her with.

"Come on, Prettijohn. 'Tis not hid in there," said Blue softly in the doorway, while I squinted to see what humped burden lay behind him in the shadowed hallway. "Come on with this!"

But he paid Blue no mind and came round the bed to stand with his square, muddy toes not four inches from the tip of my nose, till I was certain he was fixing to stoop down in a twinkling with one scarred, dirty hand and fetch me up in his clutch. He stood there a full minute, listening, I suppose, for some sound or signal from the other man

Elisha who was on the floor above, ransacking the place for whatever it was they were after.

"Come on with this here business, blast you, Prettijohn," came the man Blue's hoarse order from the hallway and I saw the boot tips turn and stride away and presently both men were gone, leaving behind the smell of the one called Prettijohn like the rank reek of a wet buffalo robe, so alien in that little room that was always so sweet with the scents of Sally and her wild flowers and sachet bags and such.

The door drifted to a ways, since they hadn't bothered to shut it, so that we could hear them still striving and grunting with their burden down the stairway and bungling it, whatever it was, because they were both middling drunk, and dropping it now and again, carrying it on a few yards and then dragging it some more and cursing and arguing softly back and forth about Elisha and his gruesome fancies. And we heard them fetch it down the stairs—*thump, thump, thump*—and there was the chinking now like a thin chain of some sort dragging behind it. They got it to the great front door at last and I judged now that there was no great secret about their cargo for when they got the thing outside they slammed the door with a great bang, though it may have been the wild wind that tore it from their grasp.

I was feeling like letting out a holler at my own bravery after having been through such a show but a glance at Sally told me it was only the beginning of it. I had risen up and was fixing to commence talking loud to her about how I hadn't really been scared at all. But Sally was sitting up ramrod straight in the feather tick, motioning me to be still.

"What's wrong now, Sally?"

"Hush, Dan'l," she whispered.

I stared at her.

"Hide yonder in the trunk by the window. And take the box with you. Oh, hide, Dan'l, quick."

"But, Sally, they've gone."

"No, Dan'l, no. There's another one still hunting. Oh, do as I say, Dan'l! I think this one's *clever.*"

"I'll hide down here behind the bed again."

"No, Dan'l. He's sure to look there. Oh, Dan, if you never do another thing I ask you—please hide yonder in the trunk! He's hunting for something, Dan'l, and I don't think he knows yet you've got it."

"What, Sally?" I said and she gave me such a face I went grumbling to it in the firelit dusk: the big, humpbacked hair trunk with its rough, brass-bound lid all bathed in moonlight. I set aside the pewter stick and heaved up the weighty lid. Then I crawled in and scrontched down there, half choking in the camphorous rolls of old comforters and Sally's ragged, herb-sweetened little petticoats and scented camisoles. It was then that I heard the voice of the other one—the one she had sensed was there. It came from somewhere off in the north end of the house, in the bedroom of old Jacob and Meg, I judged, and from the sound of it he had Turk out of bed and was bullying and ragging him around considerable.

"He had it when he come here tonight! So it's hid somewhere beneath this roof!" I heard him bawl in that queer, high voice I was to come to know all too well in the months to come. "Or else he gave it to you or your woman yonder! Who else would he give it to? It's you or her yonder! Now which is it? Tell me, Master Turk, or I'll carve the livers out of the both of ye!"

And then I could hear Meg weeping like a sheep, half

asleep and all bewildered and old Jacob was mumbling
something, too thick and babbling drunk to understand,
let alone answer, and directly the voice commenced again,
cursing all kinds of vileness, and I heard glass break and the
scrape and crash as a small chair or stool went sailing,
kicked across a floor, and then the fast footfalls came pattering down the hallway. And that was one of the two
queer things I first noticed about the sound of him: that
voice and those footsteps that pattered, not sounding like
the proper stride of a man at all. They were heavy like a
man's tread, still they sounded somehow short spaced as if
they were hobbled together by a short length of rope and
didn't have much space to run in.

In another instant the door to Sally's room came crashing wide open again and I admired to hear the way she
pretended to stir and murmur in deep sleep as he went
probing about her room. He said nothing to her; he
seemed too angry to notice she was even there and yet he
must have, for I heard him mutter beneath his breath:
"Why, no! He'd not fetch it to a child!" Though he still
prowled the room, softly, searching. And the sounds he
made in his throat—that was the other queer thing to him.
It was a choked, whining sound, a kind of frenzy of high
humming. And, like the footsteps, it didn't seem the sound
of a man, nor woman either, but rather like the chanting,
ragged whimper of an old and furious child. I was more
frightened than I had been of the other two—Blue and
Prettijohn—because I could sense something fresh and
horribly different about this other one. The first two had
seemed at least men—mortal and smelly and drunk—while
this new creature that scampered whining about Sally's
moon-bathed bedroom—it gave me the feeling of something monstrous and misshapen, born of other worlds. It

went round the room a while longer, searching furiously for something and stepping in that odd, stomping tiptoe and the sound it made inside: it was a rabid, ravening sound, like the voice of some small, unspeakable thing, frothing, struggling, within the wicker cage of itself. It seemed to stand still a spell, glaring down at Sally, I judged.

"No no. It wouldn't be here. He wouldn't have given it to a child."

And with that it went pattering heavily out and with one last vile, whining curse we heard it slam the front door behind it.

I tell you it had all shaken me up considerable and I lay there in the trunk another good quarter hour before I showed my face, even though I could hear Sally's anxious whisper from time to time: I reckon she was afraid I'd smother among all her petticoats and truck.

With a sneeze I crept out at last and gave a look at Sally. The fire had gone cold in the grate and the glow was gone and the wind howled keener in the cold chimney. The moonlight seemed brighter though and I could see the excitement in Sally's round face.

"Dan, you've got to run to Major Henthorn's house."

"In my bare feet through the snow?"

"On your hands and knees if need be. Dan, it's that box they're after."

"Be damn, I thought of that!" I cried. "I bet there's something in this chest we missed. That's what they're a-hunting, Sally. Maybe it's got a false bottom. I'll bet we'll find Pap's map hid somewheres in here yet!"

"Dan, fetch it to the Major's. *Now,* Dan! It'll be *you* they'll be hunting if ever they find out you've got it!"

"Sally, don't they know the Frenchman fetched this box to me?"

"Sure they don't, Dan. Who'd guess your pap would send it to a child? But now, Dan, go! Fetch it to the Major for safe keeping."

"Suppose they find out I'm Pap's boy?"

"It's a sharp gamble."

"Won't they suspicion?"

"They haven't yet."

"Won't old Jacob tell them?"

"He's too dumb drunk to put those two twos together," said Sally. "And Meg's too kindly turned. She'd not betray you, Dan. Not even if she guessed."

Well, I didn't much fancy leaving Sally alone but I had to allow she was right about the Major knowing what to do. And she told me where to find a big pair of beaverskin boots of hers in the corner behind the clothespress and I managed to pull them on though it was a fair tight squeeze and so was the window, for it had pretty nigh frozen shut. Still I tugged and hauled till I got it up a foot and hitched on through at last.

The cold air hit me like a waterfall. I stood a spell wondering if I dared take the old sorrel mare, but I figured I'd cause less commotion on foot so I set out. The night was suddenly soundless out there with no house eaves and vines for the wind to tune itself against: no noise but the dry whisper of drifting snow and the soft clash of the dry, long leaves of the old willow by the river road and the hushed moan of wind in the tall pine trees on the little Indian mound above Grave Creek. I judged the river pirates had all headed into Elizabethtown for some reason or other, for there was no soul in sight for miles. Figuring they'd had a good half hour's start I made off briskly down the snowy road toward the bridge.

I've heard town Indians and old trappers and keelboat-men tell of it: the crawly feeling you get about seven inches down your backbone when something or someone has set its eyes on you. But I walked quickly on, kicking through the drifts of the road. And even though I could see the recent horse tracks where they'd gone that way toward town, that feeling got crawlier and crawlier. Now and again I'd pause and put my ear to the wind, trying to hark to anything queer that might be astir out there.

Were they laying for me yonder behind those old willows?—Or maybe down amid that pawpaw thicket on the shore?

I ran a ways and walked a ways and then ran on again. My breath came harder and it stood in the air before my face like pistol smoke. And still I had that itching sense of a gaze upon me.

It was not till I reached the crossroads by the bridge that I figured what it was. I'd been so full of this night's new terrors that I'd clean forgotten some old ones. I leaned against the rough bark of the hangman's pole and thought of Barnaby's head atop it. I allowed it had been those dead man's eyes that I had fancied watching me on the road.

I thought scornfully of that old rogue's head and remembered other times when I had felt its gaze upon me: nights when I had ducked my head and hurried under this very spot where now I dared to tarry. Now I stood there thinking how long ago that evil brain had ceased to scheme, how long since crows and river ravens had plucked away its eyes, how many springs since the meadowlark had flown off with its hairs to line her grassy nest. I thought to myself: Barnaby's head will never scare me again. That thought and the cold that I could feel to my very buttons filled me full of a sudden impudent maturity, so that I had half a fancy to lift my face and stick out my tongue at the thing. I stood an instant more, bracing myself and gathering my breath for the last quick march to the Major's.

I rested my hand against the pole's rough bark. That was when I felt a drop of wetness—hot as tea—splash upon it.

And I thought quickly to myself: Why, no. That's nonsense. It's too cold for rain. And besides the new moon's out and not a cloud for many a mile.

Then I stared at my hand, seeing upon it the flower-shaped splatter of fresh blood. I made my eyes climb that pole again and when they reached the top I made them look. It was nigh bright as day in that moonlight and it seemed that I had stared for an hour before I commenced to scream and race pellmell for the bridge.

Barnaby's head was gone. And in its place stood the blowing, fresh head of Jean Tailleferre with his eyes turned back and his crucifix clenched in his teeth.

3

TWICE I dropped the box in the heaped drifts along the hillside and twice my hands found it and I ran on, numb with cold and terror, toward Major Henthorn's house. Not once did I glance behind me, though it seemed more than mere fancy that quick boot-falls fell thudding in my wake. At last when I glimpsed a candle in the window I paused for breath on the rise of land just below the big stone house and turned round. There was no one in sight. I stood a spell gathering my senses back together, not wishing to look such a picture of raddled wits when I roused the Major out of bed.

Beyond the white-topped stone fence I saw the great black iron kettle that hung in the Major's yard year round. By day there was a snapping fire beneath that kettle which was always full of a never-ending stew of venison and mutton and parsnips and the Lord-knows-what-all to feed the few hungry Indians left in the bottomlands. That was only part of the reason the Major was so hated by the settlers.

Like myself, he was an outcast, though for fairly different reasons and yet it was a kind of bond between us. I was the son of a river pirate and he was a British officer who had marched impudently into the midst of that small settlement a few months after the war was over and announced that he had come to live among them the rest of his life and watch their upstart little republic fall to pieces. He was a big man and tough as an eight-pounder and he had fended off a dozen or so attempts to burn and drive him out of the valley. A real outcast, like myself, and we never had much trouble getting right to the point of things. When he'd gotten me thawed out on the bench before his great fireplace he put the ring and spool and the scrap of paper back in the box and stared at me in the fireshine.

"It's plain enough, Dan'l," he said. "You've got here the key to a treasure."

"All that truck?"

"Tut, my boy. Your dad may have been raving mad of the fever. But there's no madness about this. It's a cipher."

"A cipher?"

And he went on to explain that poor Pap had meant these three things to stand for a secret message to the place where he had hid the treasure that he someday meant me to have. Major Henthorn had thrown his greatcoat over his nightshirt and he had clapped his white wig on sideways, yet he still managed to look uncommonly wise about the whole matter. In addition to the Major's odd notions about America and injuns he had a great contrariness about slave owning, too, and that didn't help his stock much in those parts, either. He kept no slaves but had a hired white man named Wherry and now he had Wherry fetch me a bowl of hot mutton broth to thaw me out. I sat there at the long board in the Major's kitchen and ate my soup with a great

flat London silver spoon and watched him in the light of the whale-oil lamp as he fetched a heap of books and maps in from the big room he called his library. He spread them round on the table and studied them a long spell through his little square spectacles.

"And the first thing you have to weigh out in your mind is this, my lad," he said to me gravely, at last. "Do you want it?"

"The treasure, sir?"

"Ay, my lad. Now don't stare at me all agape as if I'd took leave of my wits. 'Tis a matter for the most sober thought and one that has twained and tortured the minds of older gentlemen than you. Think what it is and think how 'twas gained. The coins may look bright and clean enough when you first glimpse them, boy, but look closer. That reddish cast—no, 'tis not the color of gold. 'Tis the tint of blood, Dan, and some of it shed by your own father. And more than likely there'll be more shed before you find it. Are you willing to see that?"

"Sir, I wish harm on no one alive."

"Not even those villains you tell me are back yonder at the Golden Sickle—murderers of a poor backslid Catholic clergyman—a villain like themselves but murder just the same! And nigh on the eve of Christmas Eve itself?"

"Sir, as I see it the treasure belongs to him that finds it."

"Ah, that's so. But do you know what twists and turns and peep-of-day ambushes may await along that ruddy road to where it lies? Do you, boy?"

"Well, sir, I want my poor pap's sins to lie buried with him. Still and all—"

"Lord, lad, look at me. I don't mean to preach you a morality your teeth are too young to chew. Still, I want you to

know the game for what it is—and study it over a spell as a
man would—as a man *should*, though I'll grant you there's
few enough who will. There's been blood shed once tonight over this chest of pointers. And if we cling to them
there may be more and it may be our own. Now there's two
roads split off here and you can follow either one. You can
consign that little hellchest to the fire yonder and let the
Devil have all shares. Or you can fathom it and follow its
bloody compass where it points."

"Well, sir, whatever we do—we'll go halves—every shilling of it. And half my share to Sally."

"Tut, boy, tut. I thank you for that. But hold—we
haven't got our eggs to market yet."

He stared at me with a kindly glint to his eye.

"Have I laid it on you too hard, Dan'l? Don't put on
such a downcast look. Don't you know I'm only trying to
warn you that this night we may be embarking on a quest
of terrible dangers? We may end up with a treasure. And
we might as easily end up with a mouthful of graveyard
dust."

"Well, I know that, sir. And I'm thinking. Still and
all—"

I swallowed hard.

"—I think I'd like a try at it."

"All right," he said and brought his fist down on the
board till the silver spoon chattered. "Then I'm with you,
lad. We must commence to move then. And I don't think
we've too much time to spare."

He spread his hands and stared solemnly across his spectacles at me.

"First of all," he said, "you must go back to the Golden
Sickle as soon as you can—back to your attic room—snoring
away as if you knew nothing."

"I know that," I said.

"They'd suspect for sure if you stayed here—much as I'd like to have you."

"Besides that," I said, "I've got Sally to look after."

"That's so, too. Do they know you came here? Were you followed, d'ye think?"

"No. There was none of them in sight. Though, Lord, I could fairly *feel* them."

"Do they think you slept through all this?"

"Elisha—he's the head of them—I did hear him scratching about the attic."

"What if he questions you?"

"He doesn't know me," I said.

"Wasn't he searching for you?"

"He was hunting for a map. If he did see my empty pallet he wouldn't know whose it was."

"What if he questions you? Can you make a bald face of it?"

"I—I reckon so, sir."

"What if he thinks you were out and about tonight?"

"I'll say my chores took me to the woodyard. Or the stables."

"Does he know you are your father's boy?"

"No."

"Ay, but what if he found that out?"

I shrugged sadly. "I don't reckon I look like somebody Pap would waste a treasure on."

"Still, we must take no unneeded chances with your life, lad."

He went to the chimney shelf and found his clay pipe and filled it, then lit it with a hot coal he held deftly betwixt thumb and finger. He sucked and puffed a spell, studying it all over and blowing blue wreaths of smoke all round himself.

"Won't Master Turk tell him that you are James Cresap's boy?"

"Maybe," I said. "If he thinks of it. But his memory's awful poorly. And he's drunk most always these days and nights. It's Meg runs the Golden Sickle and Meg would never tell. Meg, she'd be my friend if old Turk would let her."

"Does he mistreat you still?"

"He swings a good lick at me now and then," I said. "But I get quicker at ducking all the time."

"Still, what if he does put two and two together—and suggest that maybe it was you the poor Frenchman brought these clues to?"

"I tell you he most likely won't think of it. Half the time he calls me Dan and the other half I'm Tip or Bob or Billy. I misdoubt if he even remembers. His brains is scrambled, sir."

"Ay, from drink."

"That. And from fifty summers of butting fights all along the river shore from the Monongahela to Osantiville. There's hardly a keelboat bully hasn't heard tell of the hardness of that man's head—or felt it."

"Well, it's plain this man Elisha and the others—they know the Frenchman brought something to the Golden Sickle."

"It is, sir."

"And—if luck favors us—they haven't figured out that he brought it *to* anyone."

"Least of all the stableboy."

"And there's this to it," said the Major. "Creatures like

them could never imagine such a thing, I fancy—any man's handing over to another the key to a treasure."

"No, I reckon they wouldn't, sir."

"So they'll fancy his journey North was only a flight from them."

"Well, it was that, too, sir."

"Still, with no goal but escape, d'ye see? And all the treasure someday for himself. I tell you I know how such ruffians think, lad! They'll fancy the Frenchman saw the game was up and hid it somewhere in the Golden Sickle."

"To come back and fetch it when they were gone," I added, as hopeful as he that we were right in our calculations.

"Well, we'll trust it's that," said the Major. "But before you go back there, Dan'l, you must realize it's a risky game."

"I do, sir."

"These men have cut more throats than you've skinned catfish."

Wherry, the Major's manservant, fetched me an old jersey coat I'd left there once when Sally and I had come in a rainstorm for our reading lessons. Wherry—he was another bafflement to the people of the bottoms, for he was an old sergeant major who'd lost both ears in the hard winter at the Forge with General Washington. The Major and Wherry—it was a riddle of many's the hearthside argument over how these two coins came to be in the same purse.

The Major said he'd set to work unravelling Pap's cipher that very morning.

"Although," he added with a queer smile, " 'Tis assuredly a strange task to be about on the eve of Christmas."

He cocked his eye at me with another thoughtful, warning scowl.

"Mind you, lad. I hope you know that there's innocent blood on every coin we seek. *Do* you know?"

"Yes, sir. But still and all, we've shed none of it."

"That's not the heart of the thing, lad," he said, and then got so solemn and grave that he snapped his pipe stem in his fingers.

"Tut, boy, tut," he said then, clapping me on the head. "I'll preach at you no more. I'm no better than you. We're both mortal and human. No, I'll preach no more, for this is Virginia's Dominion and not St. Paul's pulpit. At least, I'm clear of one thing—that I'm not setting myself up as any less eager than you to find the treasure, Dan Cresap."

He patted my head again.

"And tomorrow night I'll have news of what the clue means, I wager," he said.

"When will we hear it—Sally and me?"

"Tomorrow night," he cried. "It's Christmas Eve, is it not? You'll both come here and I trust the unravelling of the riddle will be your Christmas gift!"

"I'm still edgy," I said. "I'm thinking they might suspicion—our coming here."

"Tut, lad. They'll have their faces in grog up to the ears, I'll guess. And haven't you two midges always come to my house on Christmas Eve? You're my children! Now back to the Golden Sickle with you, Dan. For the tricky game we're about has begun!"

The moon was gone and the wind up when I went out on the hill again—just glimmers of pearled light shining through fresh, dark snow clouds in patches of smeared violet. New snowflakes lit and melted on my cheeks and mouth and I hoped for a snowfall heavy enough to hide my tracks in the river road and up the hillside to the Major's in case the men rode back that way soon. Still it was very dark

and I went home by another way I knew—through the
woods behind the old Indian mound—for I was determined that I would not pass under the dreadful spot
again that night. Yet even up there in the thick woods, even
so far away—through snow and moonless dark and distance
—it seemed I could feel upon me the awful bald stare
of the poor Frenchman's eyes.

The hounds knew me when I got back to the inn and I
murmured and whistled low to their big loping shapes that
came down across the snowbound yard. One window of the
front downstairs room was a-quiver with ruddy lampshine
as I crept to the sill and peered across it. Jacob Turk sat
slumped and drunk in his chair, a great bleeding bruise
above his eye, which he was as like to have got from a fall as
a blow. I saw the man called Prettijohn, too, and the one
called Blue and another one who looked like some sort of
hireling, and they were all clumped around the long board
with a burning lamp and stone mugs of Tom and Jerry
between them, deep in drink and talk. Poor Meg, clutching
a cold saucepan, sat stiffly sleeping in a ladderback chair
by the pantry door, as if awaiting their gruff beck and call.
But there was no sight of the other—the one called Elisha
—because I figured I would know him on sight: a big, bullying man, I reckoned, with scars maybe or a patch. And if
he was not there, I knew he was somewhere else about the
house—lurking or spying or still hunting savagely in nooks
and crannies for what he thought was a hidden treasure
map—so I decided against chancing an entrance the way I
had left. I remembered an old trapdoor in the roof above
the attic room and near the chimney—a flat square, set
deep among the shingles and with a rusted iron ring. I had
not used it since summer when old Turk used to chase me
upstairs for a licking and I knew that tonight it would be

thick-crusted with snow, still I figured I had best go in that way. I felt out the lowest of the iron rungs set almost invisibly into the stone wall beneath the thick cloak of Virginia creepers and commenced slowly climbing into the snowy dark.

Halfway up I took a chance and clambered out onto the heavy trunk of vine which grew there and scrambled over for a glance across the sill into Sally's room. She had found a few fresh coals for the grate and the fire lighted the little room so's I could see Sally's small white chin asleep above the squares of the old apostle quilt. Then I felt my way back and set my boots solidly into the rungs again and struggled up to the gutter of the roof. The icicles I knocked loose fetched up a smart crystal clatter far below me but I made it up over the edge of the roof that was slick as cake icing. But the wind and the heat round the great stone chimney had cleared most of the snow round the trapdoor and after a few tugs I pried it slowly open.

I stood awhile peering down into my attic. It was black as the insides of a cat and I eased down, fitting the door snugly back in place above me and stood a minute in the pitch black listening to the drip of melting snow from my coat. I could see the checkerboard of blue light where the fitful moon shone now and then through my latticed window onto the floor beside my pallet. I decided against striking a light to the little stub of beeswax candle I found on the chimney ledge. The place was a shambles: I hit my shins a few good licks on old trunks and boxes that had been pitched round here and yon, overturned and flung open, and my pallet was ripped up some. Suddenly I felt all the tiredness that I'd been holding back all night and wanted nothing more than sleep. I stuffed back the stray corn shucks into the sack of my bed and felt round till I'd gotten my quilt and old blanket back and skinned out of those wet boots and the cloak and crawled into the sack with my clothes still on.

I don't know how long I slept. Curses and faint snatches of "Billy in the Wildwoods" came up from downstairs now and then and once I thought I heard Meg creep weeping through the halls, but it was all woven into dreams. I remember waking at the far end of a chime of the tall clock downstairs—four strokes like a parish-house bell buried under oceans somewhere—and even my waking up seemed part of dreaming. I wasn't even sitting up in the quilt but I could see him squarely planted there in the patch of moonlight which had shifted now a dozen feet from my pallet. It's fair strange when you wake up and know you've woken and yet what you see is pure nightmare.

I took him to be a giant of a man in a three-cornered hat who had pulled off his boots, set them upright on the floor before him, and then for some unknown reason knelt behind them. Then as he came toward me in a queer kind of scampering swagger I saw that he was an enormous dwarf. Scared as I was I almost laughed at the image of him: it was as though the floorboards were dark waters through which he came wading and yet he moved with such spider-swift alacrity that I could hear the quick, cocky strike of his cleated heels on the nails in the floor. His monstrous, thick legs seemed no longer than my forearm but they were fitted out in short fine boots of scuffed ox-blood calf and silver buckles. His clothes were frayed and smoothed some by hard times but I could tell he had once been a regular Derry Dropper: he wore a short plaid coat lined with old red velvet, with a gold coin for a top button, though the others were all brass and horn as if they'd all been gold coins once which he'd been forced to clip and spend. He wore a black cocked hat and under his chin was a loose green stock held in shape by a beefsteak bone. He stood staring at me, with his chin resting on clasped hands folded over the carved silver head of his black walking stick.

I had not moved since waking. I thought if I pretended to be sleeping he might go away, but he came closer now and stood looking down square into my face. Through half-shut eyes I saw his face clear for the first time and I think he must have heard my gasp. His face seemed the most malevolent mask I had ever seen. One great crooked tooth thrust straight out of his mouth like an oar, lifting his blue lip in a kind of fixed, perpetual sneer through which he breathed in a soft slow hiss. I braced myself to spring out the far side of the quilt and make for the roof trapdoor, barefoot though I was. Then he abruptly spoke.

"Look at this, boy!"

His voice was the high, thin sound I had heard earlier while hidden in the trunk in Sally's room.

"Looky here!" he said and he had fetched out a gold coin from his vest and held it up in a shaft of moonlight. I could see it was a gold English guinea and it winked and burned as he turned it quickly in his big fingers. Now he held it down a few inches from my face so I could see the elephant on one side and England's old mad George on the other.

"Ain't it pretty though, boy?" he whined. "Would you like it?" And he spoke in a queer, cozening tone that was somehow worse than threatening.

"What would I have to do for it?" I said, evenly.

"Why, first tell me your name, little lad," he said. "We can't talk like chums till we know one another proper. Call me Elisha. Now what's your name, boy?"

"It's Dan, sir."

"Dan what?"

"Beg pardon, sir?"

"What's your last name, Dan?"

"I was a foundling, sir," I said, crossing my fingers under the quilt. "I have no last name."

"Poor boy. A poor nameless house and stableboy. Now ain't that sad! What's your wages, boy?"

"A dollar Mexican every month."

"Pshaw now. You're joshing. And do you know what this is, boy?"

"It's a guinea piece, sir."

"That's twelve months of wages, boy. Would you like it?"

"What doing?"

"Find something for me," he said. "Something valuable I lost here in these very premises tonight. I said lost when I mean it was stole from me. And the thief he hid it somewheres 'neath this very roof."

"Well, where'd the thief go, sir?" I said bold and bald-faced. "Can't you find him?"

"Took off!" he cried, throwing out one hand in a gesture of wronged innocence. "Hid the thing here e'er I could catch his hand at it. Then stole a mare and took off in this snowstorm bound North."

"And left what he stole hid here?"

"Ay! Figuring to come back, I reckon, and fetch it when I'm gone!"

He turned and paced a foot of moonlight and then paced back, with an evil glance at the window.

"I looked all night," he said, in a tight, caged voice. "And I found nought. Then I got smart and I says to myself: Elisha Thorn, who'd know best the nooks and crannies of a place like this but the boy who works here, eh? Elisha,

I says to myself, it's a cross-and-pile chance you'll ever find that parchment on your own! So find the boy of this house and set him hunting."

"It's a—a parchment, you say, sir?"

"Maybe that," he said, scowling furiously to himself and pacing again. "And maybe a tied-up scroll. And maybe just a scrap of paper—thin enough to hide in a mouse nest. And maybe a sheet of foolscap with a map and some numbers. Such a thing as could be hid 'neath a carpet, in a cubby, down a crack."

"A map?" I said then, a little recklessly but wanting to spread the impression of my total ignorance. "A map to what, sir?"

He shot me a quick, queer, glittery look and stared so hard I was afraid I'd gone too far.

"Why, if I was to tell you that, boy," he said. "Why, then we'd both know—wouldn't we? And that might not do."

"Well," I added hurriedly, "I just allowed it would help me to know what it looks like if I'm to hunt for it, sir."

"A paper. A parchment. A scroll," he said again, grating his teeth as if struggling to keep his voice even. "Any such strange thing your eye lights upon. Anything that's been drawn or drafted upon."

And my questions seemed to have kindled some madness in his mind, for he went to pacing again and whining faintly to himself. At last he whirled on me, but his glare was over my head and into the moon in the window.

"And then again," he whispered heavily, "it may be hid in some place as simple as someone's pocket. Eh? I've thought of that. It's a tricky world, ain't it now, and who can be trusted?"

And now his eye shot down at me.

"Forget the gold guinea," he said. "There's a five sovereign piece if you bring me the name of the one who has it. Can you pick a pocket yet? Are you handy at eavesdropping, my lad?—Would a little ear-and-corner work be worth a hundred shillings to you?"

"I'll keep my ears open, sir," I said shamelessly.

I knew how furiously helpless he was but I knew, too, that he was the sort whose helplessness makes him more dangerous. And he was up here with me tonight, trying every game. Even now, as he turned to me I could see his face all re-made into a new mask of dreadful and obsequious intimacy.

"Now then it just then come over me," he said in a wheedling tone. "I just then said to myself: Elisha, you ain't four-squaring with this here lad. Why don't you square with him, Elisha? He's but a poor misused orphan and if he finds the treasure map—why, cut him in!"

"Treasure?" I said in proper wonderment.

"Ay, boy!"

"What treasure, sir?"

"The Queen of Batavia."

"Beg pardon, sir?"

"The Queen of Batavia!" he cried in that high, thin whine. "A pearl necklace so bright that first glimpses have struck men blind! A necklace worth the ransom of a Tamurlane!"

He nodded evilly, letting that sink in, while I was doing some remembering of my own of that odd name in poor Pap's poem.

"That," he went on wildly, "plus six bags of gold Spanish coin to the weight of sixty. Plus four gold bars eight by six to the weight of forty. And a sack of English sovereigns and guineas."

I nodded back with wide eyes, watching as he paced himself half into a frenzy, glancing round from time to time to a small square portmanteau he had left on the floor by the staircase. Now he turned back to me, gesturing with one pointing finger.

"Devil take the gold and coins!" he cried. "It's the Queen I'm after. Find me that map, boy, for you're the only one in this house sober or sane enough to know how to use your eyes. Find it for me, boy, and I'll cut you into the gang and you'll have a horse of your own and ride the Trace with us and be shed of this life of slops and chores forever! Find it for me, boy, and lead me to the place where 'tis hid or to the poor doomed soul who has it and I swear by the King of Darkness himself that half the gold will be yours!"

When he finished he stood in a half crouch in the full faint shine of the moonlit window and I could see the small pale foam in the corners of his crooked, quivering lips.

"But then what if, when you find it—" he whispered suddenly, "what if something whispers in your little ear to keep it all to yourself—the whole bloody hoard of it: Queen of Batavia, bags and bars and all?"

"I wouldn't risk no such a trick, sir," I said.

"No, you wouldn't—not unless you want to earn a slow, hard death by it, you wouldn't."

"I surely hope you find your treasure, sir," I said, my fingers beginning to ache I had them crossed so long and my nerves commencing to feel the strain and wishing he would be gone. I measured every word for fear of making a slip.

"Not mine," he cried furiously. "It was never mine. That treasure was never stole from me, d'ye see? It was *his!*"

And he turned and scampered off in that short-legged swagger to the portmanteau that stood on the boards by the stair. He fetched it up as if it were right heavy and carried it back to the window and straddled the same saltbox where the poor Frenchman had sat that very night. He stared at the square portmanteau between his jutting little boots and I thought I could hear him whispering to it.

"It was Barnaby's," he said suddenly, and I knew then what was in the portmanteau and I shut my eyes for a minute and wondered if I could keep from screaming if he took a notion to open it.

"My own brother Barnaby," he cried. " 'Twas his—all of it. The treasure was his because he was head of us all and because it was his pistol that killed the Spaniard that night down on the Devil's Elbow. The treasure was Barnaby's, I say! And once I've claimed it back in his poor murdered name I'll be free to set about my proper business in these counties."

"And what is that, sir?"

"Why, settling an old score, that's what," he said, fingering the brass latch of the carpet-covered portmanteau as if he half meant to have the wind-withered thing out on his knee where its rain-ruined ears could better hear.

"A score to be settled against the living kin of a devil in Hell," he cried. "The kin of him who betrayed poor Barnaby here to the Regulators that summer night and stole the treasure of the Spaniard for himself!"

"Do—do you know his name?"

"Cresap!" he half-screamed, and jumped to his little feet.

"Cresap!" he cried again, moving off with his burden in one hand and his high walking stick drumming in the other. "He has a widow! He has a child! A half-breed's rumor drifted to me last month that they're hiding out somewhere's upriver!"

He pounded the ferrule of his heavy stick on the floor till the sash weights chattered in the window.

"And I'll find them out! Oh, I'll find them out!" he shouted in that voice of ravenous fury. "And when I do I'll slaughter them each in as slow and hard and bloody a way as fancy can devise!"

He stood a minute swallowing and gasping his breath back after the effort of his tantrum and then I heard him chuckle. Before he went down the stairwell something yellow spun twinkling through the moonlight and bounced upon the quilt. He chuckled again. The cold gold guinea came to rest against my hand.

"Gold draws gold," I heard him whisper. "Sleep well, orphan Daniel. And rest up for tomorrow morning's look-and-listen game."

I lay awake a long while. I did not touch the coin. Later on as I tossed round in awful dreams of Spaniards and pearl necklaces and queens I heard the gold guinea fall to the floor and spin idly still on the boards. I fetched it up then and studied its elephant and its big-nosed king in the first blue, cold shine of day across the sill.

And by breakfast I had half a mind to tell the Major on that night of Christmas Eve that this yellow coin was every bit of this world's gold I ever wanted to see.

IT WAS almost nightfall. I crouched hidden in a musty narrow passage off the upstairs hall, listening to Sally's voice as she came singing along the hallway wall, feeling her way to her room. I had been trying to get word to her all day but somebody was always about who might overhear.

> Last night there were four Maries,
> Tonight there'll be but three
> There was Mary Seaton and Mary Beaton
> And Mary Carmichael and me.

She crept closer along the panelled wall and I got ready to signal her when she came nigh. At the risk of a licking for neglect of duties I had kept hidden most of the day in different secret parts of the house. My nose itched from dust and the sharp smell of candle smoke, but the dwarf's threat had left me shaken and I knew that my life was in more danger with the passage of every hour. Half forgotten as my Cresap origins were, there was always the chance that old Jacob Turk's gin-muddled wits would recollect and let slip my name in Elisha's presence.

> Oh little did my mother ken
> The night she cradled me
> That I would die so far from home
> And hang on a gallow's tree.

"Sally!"

"Dan? Where are you?"

"In here, Sally. To your right. Crawl inside for a spell. I've got loads to tell you."

I helped her in and we crouched there together in that fusty place while I told her all the news I could remember. I reckon it was no darker to her in there than the rest of her world, but I was looking forward to the warm lamplight of the Major's house when we could both get away.

"What time will we go?" she said.

"About an hour past candle-lighting time," I said.

"I'll be in my room," she said.

"I'll come for you. We can get out of the house through a special way I know."

"Take care, Dan. And do be careful. I feel so many dangers gathering round—like shadows. Remember, Dan, there are shadows my eyes can see that yours are ever blind to."

"I knew you were scared," I said. You always sing 'Mary Hamilton' when you're scared."

"It'll be all right, Dan," she said. "It's Christmas Eve. Nothing bad could ever happen to us on Christmas Eve."

I shivered despite myself because I knew she didn't believe that much more than I did and when she had left me I stayed awhile in the dark listening to the ruckus downstairs.

In the great common room the pirates were raising a great to-do, drinking and singing and hollering and dancing. Some rough strangers had come in from the river bottoms round about and fetched with them a pair of sharp-voiced girls and the thump of their dancing feet shook the house and rattled the windows. It was as though the knowledge that it was the eve of Christmas had brought upon them a strange, feverish frenzy. Maybe some of them had had half-normal infancies of some sort somewheres—with songs and simple gifts; or maybe they'd been so grinding poor they just envied and hated other people for such things and it was as if now they tried to banish these snatches and bits of memory from their minds. Off among the valley farms and villages folks were singing songs of the Lord's birthday that night, I judged, but not here in the Golden Sickle. For the pirates' tunes were anything but carols—rough ditties and bloody ballets they'd learned somewhere between the bawdy lanes of Pittsburgh and the wild Gut of Memphis—"Nappy-cot and Petticoat" and "Maggie Lauder" and "Billy in the Wildwoods"—while in between was the rusty whine of Jacob Turk's cherrywood fiddle in the holler and hammer of the hoedown. I came out of hiding into the shadows of the downstairs hallway and stood a spell listening.

"Tip? Bob?" I heard old Turk's voice howl presently. "What's that damned boy's name—I disremember! Where is that damned boy—Tip? Is that him yonder in the hall, Meg? Bob? You, yonder. Come in here, Tip, and wait on custom like you're paid to do."

I braced myself, thinking I'd rouse less suspicion if I showed myself around a little before taking off with Sally for the Major's. I judged that by the time we went they'd all be too drunk to notice.

I stepped into the room half expecting a cuff upside the head but no one—not even Jacob Turk himself—seemed to notice me there. It was a strange sight, that big room. The board was spread with bottles and pistols and tankards and three-cornered hats, and Jacob Turk was drunk as old Noah while Blue and Prettijohn were sitting on the long bench before the red roaring fire, each with a country girl on his knee. Jacob Turk looked square at me and seemed to have forgotten that a moment before he'd been bellowing after me. But the dwarf—who had not spotted me yet —he was the strangest sight of all. He was dressed up even fancier than the night before, with a crimson jacket of rubbed and ragged-sleeved velvet and a beaver hat and some lace at his throat, and he was in the middle of the floor, skipping and doseying about with a mean-faced fat girl a good five hands taller than himself while he sang to old Turk's fiddle in that whiny little voice of his:

> The needle's eye that does supply
> The thread that runs so true-ly
> There's many a lass that I have passed
> Because I want but you-ly.

I leaned back in the long billowing shadows cast by fire-shine and lamp and watched that strange sight. I marvelled at the swiftness of the dwarf's little legs and yet there was something awful and scary to it, too. Back on her chair by the pantry door sat Meg, as usual, watching it all with stunned and long-suffering eyes. The fat girl swung round the dwarf and flung out her freckled arm, sending a bottle of wine bursting on the floor.

"Never mind that! There's a cellar full of that and better!" cried Jacob Turk, glaring down at the mess of it like a great litter of glass and blood. "Where's that boy to fetch the bottles! Tip? Bob? Damn that boy and his eyes to Hell! Meg, where's the boy?"

"He stands yonder," said Prettijohn, as I moved out into the light.

The dwarf stopped his dance and let out a cry and waddled briskly toward me with his wild eye burning.

"Ay, that's the fine lad," he said: "That's the fine boy, Dan'l!"

He strode close and clapped me on the shoulder.

"Here's the fine boy who's going to help us all," Elisha cried. "Here's the boy who's hunting high and low for the thing we came to seek. Did ye find it yet, boy?"

"No, sir."

"But you've been searching?"

"Yes, sir. High and low."

"Well, there's still time," he said. "You'll earn that partnership yet."

"That's Tip! There he is, damn me," cried Jacob Turk, staggering loosely forward and slamming his fiddle down among the litter of the table. "That's the damned boy I pay good money to and he don't turn a hand all day. Let me have hold of him!"

"Stand back, tavernkeeper!" cried the dwarf. "This boy here's the best chance we've got! He's hunting for our treasure map."

"Never mind that!" cried Turk. "I'll treasure-map him. Let me get a hair-hold of him."

And he lunged at me with that awful swift footedness of some big men, but Elisha was quicker. He scuttled—he did not run—to the table side and fetched up his silver-chased walking stick and with a movement so swift that it looked like a bright silver feather in the light he whipped out a thin steel sword. He held the tip of it against Jacob Turk's throat till it creased in the fold of his neck and then commenced walking him backward.

"You're awful eager to still that boy!" cried the dwarf and still walking Jacob back into the brightness of the fire-shine. "Maybe you'd not want that map to be found!"

"That's not so, Elisha."

"Maybe you know something about that map yourself, Master Turk!"

"I tell you I know nothing, Elisha!"

"And why do you call him Tip and Bob—when his name it's Dan'l? Is there some secrecy afoot here?"

"You know I'd not hide anything from you, Elisha."

"Well, then leave this boy here alone," shrilled the dwarf. "He's the only one beneath this roof I trust, I tell you."

And now he turned slowly to me and the smile was half faded from his face.

"That's so, ain't it, Dan?—I can trust you, can't I?"

"Yes, sir."

"And tell me your name again."

"Dan, sir."

"And not Tip—not Bob?"

"No, sir."

"And you've got no last name, you say?"

"I was foundling, sir," I said, with my heart curdling inside me as I glimpsed a brightening scowl on Jacob Turk's befuddled face.

"I have no last name, sir," I said, with a sidelong glance at the open door to the hallway.

"Wait now," cried Jacob, his face screwed up in an effort at thought. "Wait now—that's not just so. Tip has a last name."

"What is it?" said Elisha.

Old Jacob scowled again and scratched the great bruise
on his forehead and there was no sound but the snapping
log fire on the black iron dogs and the dwarf's sharp breathing.

"Tip's last name," said Jacob. "Why, it's—it's—I disremember. Now wait till it comes to me. It's Dan—Wait
now!"

Meg's outcry was like a woman taken in a vision: it filled
the stillness and all faces turned as she lifted her wan face
and commenced in a loud, thin singsong:

> And Joseph he was a carpenter man
> And Mary she baked and spun and spun
> And when was ripe-cherry time again
> A family was begun!

"Shut your mealy mouth, woman!" cried Turk, turning
on her.

"But 'tis Christmas Eve!" she cried even louder and fell
back against the pantry door as Turk fetched her a lick
across the shoulders and cursed her some more.

"None of us here wants to hear about that!" cried Elisha
and grabbed up Jacob's fiddle and thrust it at him. "Get on
with your fiddling, Master Turk."

And Meg gave me a long, loving look and fell silent, nursing her bruise, and none of the others looked back at me
and in their drunkenness the talk of my name was forgotten. I figured it was as good a time as any to go fetch Sally
and be off to the Major's house before discussion of my
name might chance to come up again. She was ready and
bundled to the ears and as we stole out the pantry door into
the moonlit garden we could hear the high voice of Elisha
calling dance turns:

Hey Jim along, Jim along, Josie
Hey Jim along, Jim along, Jo—!

The garden was still and motionless as a painting. Snow covered the scuppernong trellises and the sleeping apple trees, and the stars and moonlight shone on the great yellow sandstone sickle set among the weeds that grew from the flagstones. The darkened sundial in the middle marked no hour, and the shadows were bunched and heaped in the winter-cold rose bushes like clots of congealed night. Sally seized my hand suddenly and drew me back before we had gotten ten paces toward the gate which led to the stableyard.

"Someone's yonder, Dan," she whispered. "Someone watching us."

"No one knows we came this way. How could they be there?"

"I feel them," she said. "I know they're there."

I pulled her back into the shadow of an old yew tree and we waited a spell, listening.

Soft and low I heard it: someone whistling the first few bars of "Maggie Lauder," a tune that the Continental Army had marched to, and a moment later the huge silhouette of a man filled the archway of the garden gate.

"It's me—Wherry," he whispered, motioning us toward him. "Major said for me to watch for you to come out of the house. He said the minute you showed your faces I was to fetch you up to the house on horseback."

Wherry was riding a calico gelding and had led a gentle roan mare for me and Sally to ride. We lit out through the snow on the hill behind the Golden Sickle—not risking the river road for fear of being seen out front—and went through the high, snowbound timber to the Major's house.

He was at the door to greet us, his big round face wreathed in smiles and a small printed map in his hands.

"Did you figure out the cipher?" I cried the minute we were indoors. "Have you plumbed out where the treasure is hid?"

"Tut tut, Dan'l. Good evening, Miss Cecil."

"But the treasure, sir," I cried. "Have you spotted it on that map yonder?"

"Never mind that now, Dan," he said, fetching his greatcoat and cocked hat and his heavy, carved thorn stick. " 'Tis Christmas Eve, my children. We will talk of treasure when the time comes. Come along now. We're off to church."

I reckon my face showed my impatience to know what his day of studying and figuring had earned him and whether or not he'd figured out Pap's message, but he wouldn't even talk of that yet. Sally was middling religious herself and among her few possessions was a Book of Common Prayer—a small, fat, leather-bound volume with the date 1603 on the title page and the English crown and Tudor rose blindtooled in its age-blackened lambskin binding. She'd get me to read to her from it sometimes: a few psalms maybe or some of the red-letter days in its almanack, but I was never much of a one for praying unless it was to get something; the only religion I ever got was from going to church with the Major when I couldn't duck it and I guessed this was one of those nights.

The Episcopal meetinghouse was a big brown log building on the river road about a half hour's ride north of there, and I didn't much relish the prospect of riding that far in such cracking cold weather. But the Major had made up his mind and, besides, I figured maybe it might swing the Almighty about to our side a little and even improve our chances for the treasure all round. Not only that, but going to that church with Major Henthorn any time was a right lively experience in itself. His popularity in that church wasn't much better than it was anywhere else among the bottomlands and he'd had to fist-fight or cane-whip about a dozen men before he'd ever gotten to go worship there at all. You never knew what was going to happen in that meetinghouse when the Major was along. He had an odd kind of notion about churchgoing—he wasn't what you'd call a religious man, but just the same he had subscribed enough money when the church was put up to own seven seats on the back bench all to himself. To himself and his family—he explained that once when I asked him about it. He said that his wife and five children were in England but that they might as well be dead for all he ever heard from them and it was his caprice to keep those six empty seats waiting in case they ever came. But they never came. And whenever the Major and Wherry and Sally and I went to meetings there were always those three extra seats in our midst, and it gave you a sort of ghostly feeling to see them and to think that even the seat you sat in belonged to some-body you'd never know—ten thousand miles away. It felt like ghosts at your elbow.

We hadn't hardly got settled in the back till trouble began. Four Delaware Indians came sidling in like wagon-whipped dogs and stood silent against the rear wall near the iron stove trying to get thawed out. They had no hats over their long black plaited hair and they wore ragged towcloth shirts and torn linsey jeans that they'd stolen somewhere or gotten in charity from some white man. Their feet were bare and swelled up and cracked so bad they tracked a little blood in with the snow when they came, and they were the sorriest, saddest lot you could fancy. The preacher that night was a one-eyed tinker named Fothergill and the minute he saw those Red Indians get all settled back there against the wall he hammered on the pulpit Bible till the crowd stopped singing.

"Forgive us, Lord," he cried. "But it looks like we're not all Christians here tonight."

Everybody turned around and stared at the Indians until those poor devils' eyes all turned to the floor and they commenced fidgeting and looking sadder than ever.

"Forgive us, Lord," cried Fothergill in a louder voice. "But it looks like this little flock needs weeding out before we get on with the praise."

I don't know who moved first: the six elders who started for the back or Major Henthorn. Whenever the Major moved to do anything he was quick, and yet he always had an air of gentleman's grace about him. He moved that way when he went over to the Indians and stood for a minute talking with his hands, and directly he led the four to his bench. Then he motioned them to sit down right next to Wherry and Sally and me. The gasp that went up in that cold room sounded like it came out of one throat, but the Major he never batted an eye and when the Indians were all seated on the bench he sat down, too. A big keelboat-man named Fitch came over and stood square in front of the Major with both fists on his hips and his legs set a yard apart.

"These critters ain't Christian, Henthorn," he said in a loud, ragging tone.

"Aren't they?" said the Major, cold as river ice. "Are you one, Fitch?"

"Now looky hyere, Henthorn!—You hain't living under the King of England no more!"

"Better than him!" cried the Major. "I live under the

King of Heaven whose birthday is tonight. Or did you also whip Him in your war?"

Fitch never budged, but when he did show some sign of heading over toward the Indians the Major and Wherry both got up and stood on each side of him.

"Them men hain't Christians!" cried Fothergill from his pulpit.

"No, they're not, Master Fothergill!" snapped the Major. "They're something a notch higher. They're what He called the Least of These."

Then he whirled on the big keelboatman and fixed him with a stare that would scorch a candlewick.

"Now, Fitch, I know you," he said. "And I know your history, too. These good people in this church tonight don't like the smell of Englishmen or Indians or river pirate's orphan. Well, I can put up with that. Now what puzzles me is this: How can they stand the stink of a Tory—and a skulking dog's coward of a Tory at that?"

Fitch flinched as if the Major had struck him, and my guess is he would have if the big man hadn't slunk back to his place on the front bench where the grumbling had been the loudest. The people seemed settled down a little, but the Major wasn't done yet.

"Master Fothergill," said he in a steady, clear voice. "This bench is my property and God's. It seats any seven people I happen to choose. And whoever those people happen to be they are my family. Now have you and Fitch yonder and a few more strong-arm bully Christians got the stomach to try throwing my family out of this place tonight? Because if you do, Wherry and I are waiting for you and I reckon young Dan here would give us a hand if we needed it, which I doubt. Or are any three of you of the kidney to go outside in the snow with me alone and have a little chat about the subject of the different stuffs that Christians are made of?"

He glared round at Fothergill and the backs of fifty necks.

"No? Well, then, get on with your Christian service, Master Fothergill, and a Merry Christmas to you!"

But the angry, stubborn silence burned like something smouldering, and when the Major got tired of silence he threw back his head and began to sing alone:

> A - deste Fi - delis!
> Joyful and trium - phant
> Oh, come ye, Oh come ye
> To Beth - lehem!

And as he sang he kept thundering time on the floor with the ferrule of his great thorn stick and the tune and the spirit of it seemed to catch on till me and Sally and Wherry were singing, too, and then a few more voices piping up from the next row ahead of us and an alto and a basso sneaking in here and there, and it kept spreading like a crown fire till the whole room was ringing with it and even the four Indians were perking up and smiling and shyly keeping time with their poor dirty hands.

"Those poor souls were freezing," I said later, when we were on our way out to the horses. "Letting them come in like that probably saved their lives."

"I don't know about that, sir," said the Major. "But it may have saved ours."

"What do you mean, sir?"

"I mean they came in to sit on my bench for another reason than to keep warm," said the Major.

"I don't savvy, sir."

"They came to warn us."

"Warn us? Of what, sir?"

"Of an ambush on the river road," he said. "Waiting to get us on the way back. Ambush by a pack of rascals headed by someone they called 'The little big man.' "

"Elisha! Then they followed us!"

"Apparently."

"Then they suspicion something's in the wind."

"It would seem so. We'll have to take a way home over the hills. Through the forest. It's an old injun trail. Wherry knows the way."

"It's a good thing we went to meeting," I said, when we were sitting safely back in the Major's library. "Otherwise we might not have known they suspicioned anything."

"That's so," said he. "And we must silence those suspicions somehow. I think I know how and I think I even know how we may even be shut of them for good. Then we can go about our proper hunt for the treasure."

"Did you plumb it all out?" asked Sally, her dark eyes shining in the firelight. "Did you figure out the clues?"

The Major fetched a lamp and set it in the middle of the table. Then he spread out the map he had showed us earlier.

"Look ye," he said. "And remember how the scrap of verse went."

" 'Queen of Batavia—helter skelter—' " I began, and then my memory bogged down.

"That's the necklace," said the Major. "Isn't that what the dwarf told you?"

"Yes," I said. "It's called the Queen of Batavia. He said it was so beautiful it had struck men blind—" And I suddenly remembered poor sightless Sally standing there and I was afraid the phrase might have hurt her feelings; I reached out and squeezed her hand.

"It's all right, Dan'l," she whispered, her face bent above

the table with as much interest showing as if she saw every detail on the map at which the Major now tapped his finger. "Go on, Major, sir," she said.

" 'Mexican cob and Spanish doubloon,' " he went on, quoting from the last part of Pap's mysterious verse. " 'Lie hidden beneath the Full of the Moon.' Now ponder that a spell, my children. That might indicate almost any place on this wide earth, might it not? For there's nowhere that the moon does not shine."

"No. It ain't much help," I said, disappointed.

"But wait," he went on excitedly. "Your pap was no fool, Dan'l lad. He was a mighty shrewd customer and that's for sure."

"How do you mean, sir?"

In answer he fetched a great quill pen from the litter of books on the table, dipped it in a little stone inkwell, and leaning close in the lampshine made a little circle and cross on a place in the map which showed the snaky shape of the great Ohio River.

"What's that, sir?" I said.

"It's a place a man might hide treasure," said the Major. "It's a place where, having hid the treasure there, a man might leave such a clue to lead hunters to its hiding place."

The map was a big printed one of "Our Half of The Colony of Virginia, That Part West of the Appalachia Mountains and the river Known as Ohio to the Border of Kentucky. Wheeling. 1797."

"Look here, boy," the Major said, pointing with the quill point. "What d'ye see on the river?"

"Small islands," I said. "Shoal places. Ripples."

"Ripples," cried the Major. "And each of them with quaint, queer names. Here, for example—Black Man's Ripple, to commemorate, perhaps, the place where some poor slave drowned. Here's another—Devil's Ripple—doubtless a bad spot to navigate because of the current. And what's this one called?—The one here inside the circle I made?"

"Moon Ripple!" I exclaimed. "Say, that sounds like we're close."

"Now ponder this a spell," the Major continued excitedly, while each of us sipped from pewter mugs a little of the boiling hot mulled cider with nutmeg and stick cinnamon which Wherry had whipped up to take the chill off us all and warm our hearts on Christmas Eve. "Ponder it, Dan and Sally, and ponder well. Suppose once upon a time a keelboat or broadhorn had gone sailing down these tricky waters—amid deceitful ripples and unexpected turns and treacherous sawyers and planters and wild, devilish currents. Suppose now that the boat had overturned and men were lost. Suppose enough lived to tell of it afterwards to the patrons in Pittsburgh or Wheeling and the patrons told the mapmaker to mark such an evil place with proper warning and name it after the tragedy. Suppose five men had been lost."

"I don't understand that," Sally said.

"Five hands," said the Major, kindly taking Sally's small hand and placing her forefinger at a point in the river while I bent close to see. "Five hands were lost, don't ye see?" cried the Major. "And hence this spot on the river called Five Hands Ripple. Now mark ye well where it's located."

"Below Moon Ripple," I cried suddenly and pointed with my own trembling finger. "Why, yes! I see it now! It's a place beneath 'The Moon.' Five Hands Ripple!"

And I suddenly began repeating from excited memory the last two lines of Pap's poem:

" 'There is no scoundrel still alive—' "

And Sally's voice joined me excitedly and we both said it: " 'Knows these lie where the Hand is at Five'!"

"We've got it! We've got it!" I cried, seizing both Sally's hands and swinging her around in the firelight. "We've fathomed out Pap's riddle! We're on our way to the treasure!"

And I felt ashamed to think that I had thought my poor pap mad and I felt marvelous proud to think how clever he had really been. The Major lighted a new clay pipe and stood by the mantelpiece watching me frolic round with Sally while he puffed blue vines of smoke round his own contented face.

"When shall we go for it, sir?" I cried at last, falling breathless into the Major's own big, hand-carved chair.

"If all goes well," said the Major, "we'll have our chance at the treasure by the Twelfth Night of Christmas."

"Hooray, hooray!" I cried again, dancing in a wild circle with Sally. "Oh, Major Henthorn, sir, how did you ever get at the truth of it all?"

He still smiled at me, though his eyes were grave and thoughtful.

"Well, I hope only this," he said. "That before Twelfth Night is past you will have learned a solemn and wonderful fact about this world, Dan Cresap. And I mean the fact about the way with Truth."

"I will, sir, I will. And that will be the fact of Pap's hidden treasure: the Queen of Batavia and the Spaniard's gold."

"Perhaps," he said. "And if you are very lucky it will be an even rarer treasure than that."

"And what could that be, sir?" I said, a little impudence in my tone.

"The treasure of knowledge that there are two levels of Truth in this life," said the Major. "One of them is the easy Fool's Truth that lies at the surface of things. And the other one—the Truth for wise men. And that one's not so easily come by, boy. Although, alas, 'tis the only one that matters. And that for one very good reason."

"Which is, sir?"

"Why, for the very reason, sir, that the other Truth is so very often a lie."

All this left me a little mystified but I was all too filled with wonder and excitement and dreams of Twelfth Night treasure to bother my mind about it and anyhow by then it was time for Wherry to see us home and we all wished each other Merry Christmas and made ready to go. When we'd got our things on, the Major came over and tucked the big folded river map carefully inside the pocket of my great-coat. And he gave me the ring to hold as a talisman. I studied him a second or two with a puzzled scowl on my face.

"Hark to me, lad, and hark well," he said then. "I'm mortal enough to hope as much as you do that we lay our hands on that bloody, rascallish trove of riches. But if we do we're going to need our wits about us. And for that we'll need to know which level of Truth was meant for us."

"The Truth is all here in this map, sir," I said.

"One Truth is," said he.

"The Truth Pap meant us to have," said I.

"The Truth he meant *someone* to have," said he.

"Still—what I'm thinking now is this, sir," I said suddenly. "Do you really think this map should be with me?"

"How do you mean, Daniel?"

"Don't you reckon you'd better keep it here?" said I. "Lest Elisha find it amongst my things."

"Oh, I daresay he will," said the Major coolly. "For

that's what we want him to do, isn't it? And tut tut, my boy, don't pull such a face at the news."

"But, sir—"

"Tut tut, my boy. He'll find the map and then we can find the treasure!"

5

WHERRY turned to me as we came down the snowy pasture slope behind the stables and the garden wall.

"Can you go it alone now, lad—miss? We mustn't show ourselves."

"We can manage," I said. "I know a secret way in. From the garden."

Whenever Wherry spoke he unloosened the thick wool cap he kept always pulled down about the two sad, tufted holes on either side of his head, and when he listened he dropped reins and cupped both hands to hear.

" 'Tis a freezing Christmas Eve, youngsters," he said. "But I can mind a colder one. Goodnight and God rest ye merry."

And as I watched him ride away I knew he had meant the season of that grinding winter when he had left his poor ears in the snow at Valley Forge.

I felt uneasy but I tried to hide it from Sally. If the river pirates had indeed followed us and if they'd really been waiting to ambush us, as the Indians had warned, then that meant that the dwarf's suspicions of me were up. I wondered how much of my secret he was really onto by now. I had told neither Sally nor the Major of Elisha's promise to hunt down and slaughter all kin of my poor dead Cresap pap once the treasure was found. At such news the Major might have insisted that the risk of Elisha's discovering my last name was too great a gamble, even for the stakes of that king's ransom we were hunting.

The great stone shape of the Golden Sickle loomed dark in the sharp moonlight but the house seemed curiously awake, and the random candle that glittered here and there at a window lit Lord knows what watching, waiting face. The stone-paved garden was beautful as if in some winter dream. The high walls cast deep shadows. The sundial was heaped with a foot-high frosting of snow like a tall, fantastic cake, and the trees and rose bushes and trellises were bowed with burdens of thick, sparkling ermine. And these cast shadows enough to hide Sally and me as I led her cautiously to the hidden entrance, which was concealed in the stone foundation above the frozen cistern. Sally and I had both known of that way of coming and going since about the time we learned to walk and I think she might have found the way in herself had I not been there. As it was, it was frozen under loose drifts which I dug away with my aching hands and I tugged at the thick little brass ring and beat noiselessly at the ice around the stone cracks for nearly ten minutes before it came loose with a grinding, gritty sigh and the steam of the warm house air inside came wisping out. The passage was black and dusty, but I knew

the way and I did not want to risk a light even though I had a stub of candle somewhere about my pockets.

As I crawled carefully ahead Sally kept tight hold of my coattails with her little hand and giggled from time to time: such expeditions always seemed fun to her and this always made me realize that, for her, even the brightest, blowing sunlit day in summer was to her poor eyes, such a lightless, tunneled journey.

Every few yards I would stop to find my bearings by listening at the panelled wall or putting my eye cautiously to one of the tiny peepholes that were bored here and there. Most of the holes were dark, since all the lamps and candles had long since been snuffed in the rooms and hallways beyond. Still, far ahead in the tunnel, I could see a single thin pencil of light which I knew came from the small hole awled through the knotty wood near the floor in the northeast wall of the great common room. And from that direction I could hear the faint scuff of boot heels and chairpegs and the bandaged, muffled rumor of men's voices. That meant the river pirates were probably back and busy at their coarse dissipations and evil, noisy Christmas frolicking. Then I caught my breath and stopped and put my hand anxiously to my coat pocket to be sure I had not dropped the Major's great, folded map. In the dark I turned to Sally.

"Sal, what do you reckon Major Henthorn meant by that last thing he said?"

"I disremember, Dan. What was it?"

"About not minding if Elisha laid hands on this map?"

She was still a spell, studying and pondering.

"Why, it's plain, Dan," she said softly. "This map he gave you—he means them to find it."

"But why?" said I.

"Because this map he gave us, Dan—it's likely not the one we saw on the table."

"But I saw him make the circle and the cross to mark where Moon Ripple is!" I cried.

"Well, then, this one is another map—and it's marked wrong to lead them a fools' chase. You mind what he said about them finding this map so we could find the treasure?"

"Well, he knows what he's about," said I. "And I reckon we must follow his lead."

Sally sighed.

"He's funny and—English sometimes," I suggested. "Maybe it was just some little Christmas joke of his."

"Maybe," said she. "Though I think he was in dead earnest. You mind what he said about two kinds of Truth?"

"Yes."

"Then this is the Truth he's meant them to have," said she. "Which is no sort of Truth at all. Just listen to those rascals in the common room. I wonder what they're up to now?"

"Let me crawl up yonder and take a peek," said I.

The gals were all gone: just the men there—old Jacob and Prettijohn and Blue and Elisha and a half dozen other mean-faced cases I'd never seen. The place was a fair shambles—benches still standing but kicked awry, and stools and split-bottom chairs upturned and flung all round, and spilled liquor standing in pools by the hot hearthstones, and busted bottles and stone jugs and trampled pewter all round the littered floor. Among them all only the dwarf seemed reasonably sober and even *his* face seemed drunk with something besides grog and he was clutching his black, silver-handled stick till the knuckles on his fists shone white. It didn't take me long to catch the wind of their argument, either, and that gave me a right good turn because they were talking about the treasure like they'd as good as found it.

"Hark to me, Jacob Turk, while I tell it to you again," the dwarf was saying in a high, even voice. "The bar gold and coins is yours to divide. But the Queen of Batavia is mine! 'Twas Barnaby that won it, wasn't he?—my blood brother whose hanged and hacked-off head lies yonder in that box by the hearthstones! And if I was to fetch the poor thing out now and face you with it I'll vow it would *swear* them pearls was mine. With his dead lips now he would tell you what was my share, Jacob Turk!"

"To hell with Barnaby's head!" cried Jacob Turk, slamming one fist on the board and shaking the other at Elisha. "Them pearls is to be sold in Savannah. That was decided on long past. And the money divided amongst us! Who says them pearls is yours?"

"I," cried Elisha. "I say so!"

"And who are you to say so!"

"I'm chief here, that's who!" cried Elisha.

And it was plain that the argument was all between the two of them, with the others hovering in a circle about the board and benches like roadside bullies at a bear baiting with Jacob Turk as the bear. Nobody spoke, nobody moved. Elisha glared round at them.

"Well, who *is* chief here then?" bawled the dwarf in a tight, raging voice. "Am *I* still chief—or would you have for chief that great slobbering sack of brags and barley named Jacob Turk?"

For a long spell there was no other sound but hard breathing and the drum of the fire in the chimney.

"Who's chief here? Who's best man in this room amongst ye?" cried the dwarf again, ranging their faces with a long, hard, sweeping stare. "Well, spit out the answer, you scum of the Memphis Gut!"

And the others muttered and shuffled and bowed their faces and turned aside, not wanting to meet the dwarf's black eyes. And presently Blue and Prettijohn dragged the board and benches back a dozen feet to make an arena for the two. At that, Elisha smiled suddenly and went deathly calm, with none of him moving but his swift black eyes and his fingers that scuttled and fiddled round the silver top of his stick.

"So it's to be *that*, me darlings?" he said softly. "So that's what's up here tonight, eh? That's the game to be settled, eh? And all along I thought it being Christmas Eve we'd all ring round the table yonder for another round of grog and a few games of 'All Fours' or 'Vingt et Un.' Eh? So it's 'Who's to be Chief' eh? Is that to be the game here tonight, my beauties?"

Prettijohn shuffled forward two paces and nodded.

"It's just time again to see who's best man, 'Lishe," he said in a sheepish voice, and withdrew.

"We'll all vote on it," cried Blue. "After you and Turk yonder has battled it out."

"That's right, 'Lishe," cried Prettijohn. "Since we've all nigh got our hands on that treasure—it'll save disputin' later!"

Elisha grinned more evilly than ever and, with a sound like a scythe in dry wind, he twisted the silver handle and flicked from his hollow stick three feet of thin blue steel that looked like a stiff silk ribbon and thin as a rush of river cane. He stood with it in his hands a moment flexing it back and forth like a bow and staring at Turk in cold contempt.

"I could slice you down like cold meat before you could

whisper Mercy," he said hoarsely. "But I want this show-down to be *even!*"

And some of the strangers there snickered at that: the notion of an even fight between the dwarf and big Turk. But they all fell still as Elisha turned and flung the sword like a spear so that it whanged into the panelling and through it a few feet above our heads and stood buzzing in the stillness like a Jew's harp. Then he turned back and stood sneering at Turk, who had now risen and peeled out of his shirt and stood there with his big chest sweating in the light.

"*That* thing yonder!" Elisha cried shrilly. "You want *that* thing for chief! Is that it? So you're tired of a stum-bling freak like me for your head—is that it? And you reckon *that* thing yonder is bigger than me? Well, he's long, I'll grant ye—but legs and wits is separate matters! You want Turk for chief? Why, you poor trash rakings of Knoxville, don't you recollect the night down in Shawnee-town I killed two men in the lane back of Big Nancy's to settle this selfsame matter! Do you fancy I can't handle *one* of him yonder?"

"Come on and try, 'Lishe!" cried Jacob Turk in a chok-ing, furious voice.

"G'wan to it, Jacob," called one of the strangers. "That midge can't lay a hand on you!"

Jacob Turk was a head fighter and the hardness of his head was famed from the Monongahee to Poverty Point. The odd fact was that he was never much of a show with his fists, although his hands were powerful and quick to drag a man within butting range. He had split the skull of many a drunken rafter or keelboatman and it was claimed once he'd even whipped the awful Colonel Plug and fought Mike Fink to a draw. When there was no one around to fight it was his custom to amuse himself making bets, with river travellers and gullible drummers, that they couldn't hurt his face with their fists. That neck of his was swift as a snake and when the strongest man swung at Jacob Turk's nose Turk would duck his head an inch or two and take the blow full in the brow, which usually broke most of the bones in the other man's hand. Now he raged at the dwarf, readying himself, working himself to proper pitch.

"Come on now, you dram-sized frog!" he bawled and jumped in the air to click his heels and crow like a rooster. "I'll pluck ye apart like a well-roasted fowl, you waddling, half-pint freak!"

Elisha took all this so cool and unruffled that it made all eyes round glisten, and directly men commenced muttering and turning to slap coin on the board, making bets while the two squared off. Then Elisha did a thing that clapped silence down upon them all, when he walked round the table and fetched back the portmanteau I had seen in his hand the night before. It seemed none of them breathed as they watched him snap up the carpet-covered lid and lift out the dried, dread thing inside.

He stood then a long silent while, handling the head of his brother with slow and gingerly respect, brushing back its black, ropy hair from the sockets where once the eyes had been, and murmuring to it all the while in a soft, whining whisper as he set the thing upright and facing them all on a stool beside the hearth. The firelight shone dull on the taut leather of its pinched and time-darkened skin. And the strangest thing of all and, in a way, the most awesome, was that the fireshine, striking the blunted profile just so, and a ray of lampshine from the board to the right of it gave the devilish, dead face a curious aspect of animation. The eye-holes were shadowed and empty, all knew, and yet they seemed merely deepset and brooding and the withered brow seemed furrowed in thought and the strangle-bared teeth shone in a grimace as if air already was gathering in the hewed-off throat to shout the contest on.

"Now then," whispered Elisha, stepping back. "That's proper and fitting and it makes up fair count! Eh? I reckon there's five live men here to throw in with poor Turk yonder, who is about to learn the last hard lesson of his miserable, drink-drowned life! That's five for him. Now, ain't there four who'll stand for Elisha Thorn? Prettijohn? Blue?"

"Ay, 'Lishe!" grumbled a broken chorus from among the circle. "We're with ye!"

"That's four!" cried the dwarf. "And Barnaby here makes five! And ain't it fitting that he be here to see the downfall of yonder great blustering fool. Didn't Barnaby always claim it was Turk yonder who was first to run from any sort of fight but a butting? So it's fitting that he see the end of it!—eh, me lads? Barnaby, he's staring at Turk right this minute—look ye! Can't you read it in Barnaby's face that he knows who'll win? Look at his eyes, boys. Look at them, Master Turk. Can't you see that he knows you for a turntail, fatgut, runagate coward whenever it come to a real fight where it was every man stand and fight and let the hardest fend off! Can't you hear Barnaby whispering yonder, Turk? He's a-saying you're good as done for, Jacob! Eh?"

Throughout all this Jacob Turk stood staring—slack-jawed and with his face so bloodless and sweating that it might have seemed to some that Elisha's stand was already won. Rivermen are a superstitious lot, at best, and scarcely a murdering rascal among them who didn't put stock in omens, spirits and haunts. Indeed, the unflinching stare of the hanged man's head seemed to shiver the nerves of many there that night who fancied, as they must, the likely noose that awaited at the end of their own lives' scurrying race.

And Turk, who had shaken off most of his drunkenness by now and some of it from shock looked slow at gathering himself back together. But then it appeared that the sight of the head, which had awed him at first, now seemed to strap him on to fresh new fury. And yet it was a curious, unsettled kind of rage. He tore his eyes from Barnaby's head and glared at the dwarf.

"Damn your eyes as dead as his, Elisha Thorn!" he roared, and snatching up a stone mug of rye whisky from the board he drank it half down.

And then he crouched and went forward in a strange, squatting tiptoe toward the stool upon which the head sat glaring. When he was a yard off he stopped, still crouched and bouncing a little on his toes. Suddenly with a wordless cry he swung the half-empty vessel round and flung the remainder of its amber contents full in the dead man's face. For a short spell the whisky dripped in the stillness.

"There's a dram or two of good Monongahela for you, Barnaby," cried Turk in a hoarse voice. "Wherever your stomach is gone to—maybe that will steady it to watch your brother's skull laid open!"

And he stood up then and turned in one movement and flung the stone mug with all his might at Elisha. It went high and wide to burst on the panelling near where the stick sword still stood quivering, and when it struck it knocked down dust on the inside wall all over the heads of Sally and me.

"Come on in, Elisha!" Turk roared, and crouched, spreadlegged and bowed, with his bull head ready for the charge. "I'm a half-man and a half-alligator and who are you to fear who ain't but a half of a-nothing at all!"

And then in the rallying stillness that filled the common room Sally sneezed.

For a spell nobody moved and it seemed as I watched them that none in the room had heard. It was a frail, faint sound but clearly a sneeze and not such a one as any of those coarse noses would have made. And echoing as it did from deep behind the wood it must have had a faintly ghostlike ring.

"Is somebody yonder in the hall?" shouted Prettijohn.

"No. It sounded like it come from behind the wall yonder," said Blue and I watched through the hole as he crept fairly toward me and crouched and felt round the baseboard and his face scanned the knotty wood of the panelling and once his search stopped square at the hole, and for a moment it seemed we stared eye to eye.

" 'Twas a mouse in the wainscotting," said Blue, rising after a bit. "Get on with the fight."

" 'Twas the wind," said another. "Come on and let's be done with it!"

"Then, be God, it was a sneezing wind!" cried Jacob Turk, who was having none of these earthbound opinions.

Indeed, it may have been in that moment of Sally's sneeze that Elisha gained the edge in the contest. For now Turk had stiffened a little and straightened from his fighting stance and something was gone from his face and something new had replaced it. Slowly his eyes moved round and then his face turned to catch up with his gaze, which fixed on the thing that stared at him from its three-legged stool by the hearth. He seemed then aware that his thoughts might be read and he simpered a little with a glance round at the circle of men and squatted to fight again, trying to pick up where he'd been before he heard the sound.

"What's wrong, Master Turk?" said Elisha, slyly. "Have you never heard a dead man's sneeze? 'Twas the whisky you fed him. He may want more!—Or is it you whose nerves want steadying, Master Turk?"

Turk charged then and it all happened fast and I would have wagered no Yankee dollar of mine, nor a Spanish one either, that the contest would have been over in such short order. Turk misjudged his run because he had fought all his life with men his own height. As he went past, the dwarf's stout, short boot flung twinkling out and sent the big man sprawling and cursing among the chards and mess on the floor.

"Watch out for his legs, Jake!" cried one of the men.

"His legs, Turk," echoed another. "Them legs of his is lightning, Jake."

Turk wasn't hurt, but the fall, like the sneeze, had unnerved the simplicity of his wits and suddenly he had grown reckless. Everyone seemed to know that once Turk had Elisha in his hands he would lift him swiftly to that single shattering blow of his brow and the fight would be over.

"His legs!" yelled a voice. "For God's sake, Turk, fend shy of them legs!"

I could not imagine what they meant by this, for I had never seen Elisha fight as doubtless they had, and again and again they shouted the same warning. They seemed the shortest legs a man could imagine and yet they were swift as sunbeams and powerful, I judge, from years of clutching a saddle.

"Now then kill him, Jake!" cried a man as Turk sprang suddenly in and had Elisha in his grasp and swung him up in the air as easy as a good-sized boy.

"His legs!" they all shouted then. "Look out, Jake. The legs!"

Turk's head had already flung back before it flung forward and the movement was quick as a whipcrack, but Elisha's motions were quicker. In the very instant that Turk tossed him up Elisha had reached high and caught stout hold of a rafter and in a twinkling—almost faster than my eye could follow—both his little legs reached up like fingers and wrapped round Turk's big neck.

"Them legs," groaned a voice. "It's all up now!"

Now the rest watched breathless. And even as Turk swung gasping round and round with the dwarf circling in the firelight like a terrier locked in the throat of a bull, the men seemed to sense it was all very nearly over and one even started quarreling as another turned and began plucking up his winnings.

Elisha hailed his own victory in short, fearful shrieks and with each outcry his vicelike grip seemed to tighten, while at the same time he skillfully shielded his face from Turk's big hands which struck and tore at him as they circled. Presently however he had swung round till he hung down Turk's big back and those hands were powerless to touch him now.

"It's all up, I tell you. Give me my sixpence!"

"No, wait!"

"It's done, I say! Turk's finished. That's mine—that penny-bit's mine!"

Even as they quarreled over the money, Turk's face was turning blue and his white eyes started staring from his face and presently his legs went to buckling. As he knelt now, as if in some savage prayer with the pilgrim's burden of the dwarf on his back, and with his breath coming long and rasping, Turk's hands clawed the air above his shoulders aimlessly. Then it was over.

"Now who's chief!" cried Elisha in a final scream and gave his short body a mighty twist and Turk's neck snapped like a stick.

Later that night—in the earliest hours of Christmas morning—Turk's widow Meg packed up and fled. We were never to see her again and more than merely missing her crude kindness we felt the keenness of being alone in the house with that now somehow more murderous throng.

As for me, it was hard to grieve very much over dead Jacob Turk: he had beat me too often and too senselessly for that. And I could not escape the realization that his death and Meg's disappearance had removed the likelihood that Elisha would ever discover my Cresap identity. Still the fact that they'd followed us to church that night plus what I'd heard and seen at the peephole proved one thing and that was that something had made the pirates feel the treasure was close at hand. The words leading up to the fight had proven that. Although I couldn't know yet how much they had guessed of what Sally and me and the Major knew.

It was long after the last candle had burned down and the house of drunkards and dreamers grown still that I returned to my attic room. Almost as soon as I cleared the last step and reached for the stub of candle on the chimney ledge I heard the stir of a boot in the darkness. I had expected that Elisha would be waiting for me there. Then I saw the flash of a flint and the swell of yellow candleshine, but it was not Elisha's face that stared at me there. I sucked in my breath and stared back in astonishment. It was a girl. She was middling tall, and the round slimness of her could not hide her strength, which was clearly Indian, in part at least. She was pretty, too, with eyes quick and black—the color of pokeberries with green glimmers of lightning in them—skin hued olive with hints of her mixed blood, and high cheekbones that slanted her dark eyes slightly. When she spoke or smiled her white teeth flashed between her pretty red lips, and though she seemed pleasant enough, there was the sense in her of a quick, hidden temper, ready like a knife concealed beneath a cloak.

"Don't hunch up to run," she said. "I'll not gobble you alive. Not yet—anyways."

"Who are you?" I whispered.

"Never mind about that. My name's Barbara. But never mind about my name. It's your name that matters, youngling. There's a man I know who'd give a lot to know your name."

"You don't know—my name," I mumbled and scowled, scared.

"Maybe I do and maybe I don't, Daniel—," she said, smiling, "—Cresap?"

I shrugged and slumped down real dejected, seeing that part of the game was up, and she gave a big grin and nodded.

"Ain't that so? Dan Cresap?"

"It's so," I said. "And I'm a gonner if they ever get wind of it—them river pirates who now lie drunk and snoring down yonder in the common room. Especially Elisha."

"Elisha!" she cried with a toss of her curly black hair. "That river crawdad."

"He's a terror," I said. "I seen him choke a man dead tonight."

"And so did I," she said. "I was standing not three feet away. But don't you think I can't wrap him round my little finger as easy as pie? He's no terror. He's a pint-sized bully and a blusterer, that's all."

"Well, he's got them river pirates all buffaloed."

"River pirates!" she crowed. "That scurvy pack of turn-tail rummies and bobtail trash rakins. River pirates. What do you think I am, lad! Take a good look at Barbara, boy, if it's river pirates you want. I've ridden the Trace from Nashville to Natchez with that scum for a year now and there's nary one I'd fear to stand against."

She was a pretty thing and I remembered now her face amongst those that thronged round to see the fight. She had dressed as a man then and since they all had long hair it didn't show different, but I did remember one with a tawny, oval face that did somehow look softer than the rest. She had on the best finery she owned now, I judged—her black boots shone out from under her long loose skirt of nutmeg-colored linsey and she wore a high bodice and a jacket of red velvet with a yellow ribbon in her long flying curls.

"Barbara," she said. "Since we're going to be together a good deal you can call me that. I'm wed to that creature you're so a-feared of. Hah, that squatty little hoptoad, Elisha."

"He's your husband?"

"You could call it that," she laughed with a flash of pretty white teeth. "And that will serve for a spell. Still, it's not that I come here to talk to you about, Dan Cresap. It's about that map."

"What—map?" I said, figuring to feel her out a little more though I knew it didn't much matter whether she got it or not.

"Now don't play games with me, Dan'l," she snapped. "Or I'll slap you good. Elisha suspicions you already."

"I figured he does."

"And it's only me that stands between him knowing who you are and knowing no more than he should."

"What do you want?"

"The map," she said. "Do you see this pretty neck of mine? No. You're too young to notice such things. Well, it's a nice neck, they tell me, and I'm fair fond of it. Now, there's two things made for that neck and I'm bound to see one go round it and not the other. One is a hangman's noose. And the other is a rope of pearls called the Queen of Batavia. Is that plain? Now you've got a map that shows where that necklace lies."

"How do you know?"

"Because that chum of yours the Major is no fool," she said. "We followed you and the gal there tonight."

"How do you know he gave me the map?"

"Mainly because I see it peeking yonder from your coat pocket."

I fetched it out with a sigh and set about putting up a big show of how sore and sad I was to be losing it. I held it out to her.

"The Major sure is going to be mad when he finds out I lost it," I said with a careful sigh.

She took the map and spread it instantly in the candle-light and dropped her dark hair as her face bent and she went to tracing the ink markings with the pretty tip of a finger and chuckling to herself.

"Ha," she cried. "This looks like it might be it."

"It is," I said, putting on a big sad face and shaking my head. "It looked for a spell there like me and the Major had our hands on a treasure. That's it, all right. That's the map."

"Well, we'll see," she said. "Because there's liable to be maps and maps."

"Well," I said. "There's only one. There was only one from the beginning."

"No," she said. "There was *none* from the beginning. No map at all. Your pap wrote the secret down in cipher. There wasn't no map till tonight."

"Yes," I said. "That's so. But how do you know all that?"

"Because I was there when he made it," she said. "But I never told Elisha that. He chased the Frenchman North thinking he had a map. But we had to wait till there was a map to find. Still, that's a secret that's only known to me— and you."

"Well, it's yours now," said I. "You and the rest of them can go find your plagued treasure."

She stared hard at me with her head atilt and a bright, savage twinkle in her eye.

"There's liable to be maps," she said. "And maps."

I tried to put on a puzzled look, but I reckon I just managed to look sheepish and I wished the Major was there, for he'd know how to handle a cunning creature like her.

"That's the map to where the treasure lies," I said. "Now you've got it. Now you and Elisha can go and find it."

"Not me and Elisha," she said. "Not me and any of the rest of that roomful of stinking scoundrels."

"Just you alone?" I whispered.

"Me and you," she said, and fetched a pistol out of her belt and cocked it in the candlelight and rested it on her knee. "Don't quail," she said. "I'll not shoot you. Not unless you try to run away."

"What do you want me for?"

"Because we're leaving here tonight," she said. "You and

me, Dan Cresap. We're taking two horses and riding out of here before the moon rises—before those scum downstairs wake up. I mean this neck of mine to shine with those pearls before the new year comes. I mean to have that Spaniard's gold in my saddlebags, too. And I mean for neither Elisha nor any of that pack of trash to have a cracked shilling of it!"

"But why are you taking me?"

"Because I know you're the light of that English Major's eye," she said. "And I know he'd give up anything to keep you alive."

"Alive?"

"Ay, alive," she said. "I'm taking you for ransom, Dan Cresap, just in case this map is the wrong map and the right map's in his hands."

She lifted the long, heavy pistol in her small hand and nudged me on the arm with a gay-hearted chuckle.

"Up, Dan Cresap!" she cried softly. "And down those steps ahead of me. And don't make a sound till we're on the road and away. If you dare raise a hue and cry and they find us—well, we're both done for. Remember that."

"I'll keep still."

"Can you ride a horse?"

I nodded. "Where are we riding to?"

"Why, where the map points," she said. "And if we ride the river ice instead of the snowbound roads we should be to Five Hands Ripple before the rising of the moon!"

6

SHE WAS such a cool article; I took her at her word. Except for poor Meg I had never spent much time around women and so I wasn't much judge of their moods, but there was something about this one that made me go easy. The long silver pistol was cocked and it seemed to rest familiarly in her slim hand as a kitchen spoon might fit the fingers of some farmer's wife. She had wild dark eyes that made me reckon she might be part Mingo or Shawnee, and the skin of her high-boned face was tawny as milk and coffee. The more I studied her the more I got the feeling I'd rather it had been the dwarf facing me there over the dancing candle flame, for at least he was male and I'd have had some clue of how to deal with him.

"I mean to have those pearls," she said again, glaring off into her reflection in one of the windowpanes. "And that's the only rope that'll ever hang round this neck!"

And I knew she meant it; it was plain she wanted that

necklace even more than he did, and I judged that, when it came to getting it, she was capable of outdoing Elisha in sheer, fancy orneriness.

Still, like most boys will do with a grownup who's in charge, I poked and teased at her some, trying to gauge how far I could really go with her. And it seemed important to stall enough time to think what I could still do about it. She fetched up a harsh stare directly and waved the big blue muzzle at me.

"Come on," she said. "You're lolligagging, boy. Fetch your boots and cloak and bundle up, for it's a cold night and a two-hour ride to Moon Ripple. Haste now. Don't lag there! The moon will be up any time now and we've got to make it downstairs and out past those snoring drunkards!"

I still fussed and straggled some about getting dressed, whilst racking my mind for some solid plan to get away from her and fetch Sally and flee to the Major's. It seemed a hopeless idea, I'll grant, but all my instincts were bent on it, for I didn't much cotton to being in the grip of this wild she-creature when she found out the map was false anymore than I could stand the idea of Sally alone in the Golden Sickle with a wild horde of drunken river pirates.

"Would you shoot me if I broke for it?" I said suddenly, with a sidelong glance at the candle.

"I would," said she, without looking at me; she was admiring her white neck in the broken image of the windowpanes as if she fancied the pearls already glittered and shone there upon her breast.

"That might fetch Elisha," I said slyly. "And then you'd have to share the map."

"What map?" said she, cool as a squire. "He'd never know there was a map."

"But if you shot me for it?" said I.

"Fiddlesticks," said she. "I shot you because I found out your name. And he'd bless me for killing a Cresap."

I bit my lip and tugged on the remaining boot and fussed around getting into my cloak. I could see she was a harder case than I'd judged but, for all that, still a woman and I'd never been around women enough to let one really buffalo me. I kept glancing little sneaking looks at that candle flame.

"Supposing," said I, "that map ain't a true one?"

"Supposing it ain't," she said. "I already supposed that. And if it's not—then I'm holding you for ransom for the true one."

The only thing on my side was my knowledge of the house: I could have run headlong through every inch of it, had I been blind as Sally, and never stubbed my toe. And I knew ways, secret ways, that she had never dreamed of: ways along which I could clamber and crawl from sunup till dusk and never be glimpsed in hallway or chamber. And yet I knew there was no way from the attic to Sally's room but down yonder staircase and pellmell through the naked, candlelit corridor. She was watching me steady now, her dark eyes twinkling a little with suspicion, I judged, as if she knew I was weighing my chances.

"No tricks now," she said. "Are you ready?"

I was ready, to be sure, with my heart in my mouth as I stepped hard on a board which I knew would give out a loud squeak from the shadows a dozen feet behind her. In that instant she turned and I slapped out the candle. As I fell I realized that she had meant it: I saw the light on her furious face as the hammer struck flint and the pistol misfired and I scrambled through the pitch dark for the stairs. She stumbled somewhere behind me—across the saltbox, I judged—and made some mad girl sounds, but by the time

I'd reached the hallway I heard her boots upon the steps. It was a strange pursuit: both of us trying to make as little sound as possible because she still wanted all shares of the treasure for herself, and it was not to my fancy to rouse the sleeping rogues.

There was no candleshine in the corridor, the one light at the far north window had long since guttered and gone out and I had the darkness for friend.

"Sally! Sally!"

I whispered her name hoarsely as I pellmelled down the darkness toward her door.

"Sally?"

The moment I saw the thin bar of fireshine across the smooth boards of the hall floor I knew that Sally's door was open and that meant something was amiss. The girl Barbara's boots stampeded dimly somewhere behind me at the long hall's head and yet I knew that any instant she would see that thin light and come searching there. I peered inside and saw the shambles of the place: the quilt pulled straggling across the rug and the upturned litter of the horsehair trunk. And even as I drew in my breath I heard Sally's scream in the house below as if from the deeps of a well. I pulled her door shut to kill the little light it gave into the hallway and stood stock-still against the panelled wall trying to gather wits enough to move. It was not till then that I realized how near the girl Barbara had come. I could hear her boots whispering stealthily down the hallway along the opposite wall.

"Boy? Dan Cresap?" she was whispering. "I know you're about."

I tried to keep from breathing and that made it seem as if my heart beat all the louder and I pressed myself flat as a tick against the wood.

"Dan'l? Listen to me. We'll go shares. Can you hear me? I know you're hiding round about."

And I could hear the sounds she made as she fidgeted with the pistol, priming it again and cussing softly under her breath at the lack of light and then cocking it softly in the stillness.

"Dan'l? Shares, I say. The Queen for me and the gold for you and your chums. How's that sound, boy? Listen to me. I know you're about. Damn you, boy, hark to me! Shares!"

She had crossed the hallway now and she came past so near to me that the sleeve of her greatcoat brushed my hand and I know that if she had been a man who'd ever hunted she'd have sensed me. I gritted my teeth till my jaws ached and prayed she wouldn't hear the big drum of my pulses and in a moment she had stolen on past. I stood still yet, listening as she went whispering off slowly up the hall and I thinking of how I could get to Sally. I could hear Sally crying now and the sound of it was as if she were drowning somewhere in a great depth of sea and I in a dark boat above her. I tried hard to think of a prayer to say and all I could summon to mind was the great long English grace Major Henthorn used to say at suppers and that didn't seem to suit. Still I figured the Lord wouldn't be too particular in a squeeze like this so I gave it a try and I hadn't gotten past the part about blessing President Jefferson till I remembered the secret way from the upstairs hall to the space in the wall from which Sally and I had witnessed the dwarf's strange murder of old Jacob Turk.

"Dan'l?" I could hear Barbara whispering and the sly step of her boots as she came back the way she had come. "I know you're here somewhere. Listen to me, boy. We can be chums, you and me."

And she had come to Sally's door now and must have

glimpsed the thin bar of fireshine above the jamb, because she eased it open and stood for an instant peering within and herself all lit with the thin gold light from the empty room.

"Are you there, Dan'l? I mean to be your chum."

I could judge how much chum she meant to be now because she had stuck the pistol back in the thick belt she wore and she had pulled out, ready and open, one of the ugliest looking case knives I'd ever laid eyes on. I judged she figured that was a good way of doing away with me without making any uproar over it. I could hear Sally crying softly still and I crawled swiftly along the wall, feeling for the hinged panel. It made the softest sound in the world when it swung in but it was enough to reach Barbara's ears because even as I slipped inside I saw her face in the door to Sally's room and heard her boots spring into the hallway. Luck was with me though and I made it; and as I crawled off in the dusty blackness of the shallow corridor toward the ladder I could hear Barbara's muffled voice, above and beyond me, so angry now that she was sobbing between cusses.

I couldn't help remembering as I went hand over hand down the rungs of the secret ladder the thousand times I had gone that way when the stakes were no higher than a rainy day's game of hide-and-seek with Sally. But now as I came within hearing of the common room I knew that a much rougher sport than that was being played out. It had been such a little while since Sally and I had crouched hidden there in that space behind the peephole that some small, faint fragrance of her lingered yet.

The sight that met my eye was more macabre than before. Elisha stood warming his tails before the fire while Blue and Prettijohn lounged drunkenly on the long bench

by the board and Sally with her face in her small hands
crouched shivering on a stool between them. She appeared
unharmed though it was plain that they had been at her
with words in some way or other. Not ten inches from the
hole through which I saw it all had been set upon the floor
the rough head of hanged Barnaby, facing the party with a
mug of toddy at his ear, his rude, wind-ruined hair standing
round like rough, twisted hempstrands so that all I witnessed
there seemed framed within its wiry halo. Upon the festive
board, face up and stiff, lay the body of dead Jacob Turk.
His big hands had been roughly composed across his up-
thrust chest and big Indian pennies set upon his dead eyes,
though one dead eye stared baldly sideways at the firelit
assemblage where the coin had been jarred away. Candles
standing in the necks of empty brandy bottles burned at his
boot heels, and just beyond his twisted-awry head and upon
his towcloth shirt breast, as if in mockery of all decency as
well as season, lay the sprig of Christmas holly which Meg
that very nightfall had nailed upon the great front door.
Beyond this, in the shadows cast by fireshine and dead-
man's candle, lay sprawled round about, like loose-flung
phantoms, the sleeping figures of the others.

"I say let the gal be," said Prettijohn. "And go upstairs
for the boy."

"Ay, me, too," cried Blue. "I've got a way of asking him
questions with a coal from yonder hearth. And when I'm
done asking he'll answer or be blind as yonder gal."

"I say let the gal be, 'Lishe."

"Tut!" cried the dwarf impatiently. "Let me think.
What do you say, gal? Shall we fetch your little chum down
the stairs by the hair and let Master Prettijohn put these
questions to him? Would you like a little blind chum, little
blind gal?"

"I say go for the boy," Prettijohn said again.

"Well, one of them knows," said the dwarf evenly. "For they were both there at the Englishman's tonight. And what would they hie themselves off to him for in dead of night if not for news of treasure and maybe even the reading of some map?"

"The boy—he'll know," Prettijohn said. "Heed me, 'Lishe. No good luck can come of badgering this here gal."

"Why?" snapped the dwarf. "Would you protect her little snivelling innocence?"

Blue stirred and knocked off his mug with a smash and spill.

"Bill's right," said he. "My mom she told me that all blind souls is witches. 'Lishe, I say no good luck can come of keeping after this here blind gal. And, be God, it's luck we all want if we're to lay hands on that trove!"

"You superstitious fools!" cried Elisha. "What's eyes to do with it? Or God knows you fools would be witches, for you're blind enough, that's plain. Lift your head, little fancy lady. Come come!"

Poor Sally was brave and staunch as I knew her to be. She lifted her tear-stained cheeks and faced them.

"Now then come here, gal!" cried Elisha, with a sharp clap of his hands. "I think we've used you all wrong. Come now! Give us a tune, Master Blue! Little Lady Lamps-out likes to dance, I'll wager! Music and a dance, Master Blue —that might fill her wits with dreams of fancy places and times to come. Up now, Lady Lamps-out!"

And while Blue twanged a strange and whining quadrille kind of tune on his Jew's harp, Elisha made poor Sally dance round him with her trembling hand held high while he led her in some coarse burlesque of a minuet. I almost cried out at the horror of the sight: dead Turk yon-

der on the board with one glazed eye staring sidelong at the
dancers and Prettijohn gawking on drunkenly and all the
sleeping revellers passed out and slumped yonder in the
red and yellow shadows like creatures in some parson's
proper Hell and then Prettijohn warming to the stamping
of the dwarf's mincing footfalls and commencing to clap
his hands in time and all of it fringed in the standing, firelit hair of hanged Barnaby's head. Sally was half a head
taller than Elisha and as he spun her round she kept her
face flung up as if her blind eyes might somehow glimpse
him and after a spell of this she suddenly gave a loose, sad
cry and fainted dead away upon the floorboards.

"It's true," said Elisha presently, staring down at her
with pursed lips. "We're wasting time with her."

"Shall I go up and fetch the lad?" cried Prettijohn.

"Tut, tut!" whispered the dwarf with a wave of his hand.
"When we're done with the gal we can fetch the boy."

"But, 'Lishe, you said the time was wasting with the
gal."

"Ay," said the dwarf, smiling. " 'Tis wasting—the way
we been putting the question to her."

He stooped by Sally's side and stroked the dark hair
back from her face where it had fallen tousled.

"Firstly, we'll bring her round," said he directly, and
went to slapping her smartly across the cheeks. "And then
we'll put the question to her proper."

"I say let the gal be, 'Lishe," said Blue, in a whining,
hangdog tone. "To devil a blind gal is running plumb in
the face of Luck."

Instantly Elisha sprang to his feet and stood glaring up at
Blue.

"I'm master here!" he cried. "Or wasn't that settled
when I snapped the gullet of Jacob Turk yonder?"

His eyes swung down to Sally, who had sat up and was groping miserably round her now.

"Now, we'll put the question to Little Lady Lamps-out here in a proper way," he whispered in a voice like ripping cloth.

"What do you want of me?" sobbed Sally.

"Just this," said Elisha with his fists on his little hips and his squatty boots set apart. "It's a plain matter and wants putting plainly. And will you stand up in my presence! Do you fancy because you're half a hand taller than me that you can be short on respect?"

Sally scrambled to her legs and stood facing him, trembling some but steady-lipped and brave.

"I'm sorry, sir. I was quite unable to see you."

"Then you can hear me," said he. "And I counsel you to hear me well. Last night there was a secret fetched here to this hostel—the secret to a treasure. At the first it wasn't plain to me into whose hands that secret fell. Then you and that scullery boy upstairs went scampering to your Englishman."

"It's Christmas Eve," said Sally. "We always—"

"Tut, missy. There's more to a cat than its tail."

He gestured toward the slumped shadows beyond the board.

"One of them sprawled snoring yonder," said he. "One of those worthies spied in at a certain window. A map was seen to pass into certain hands. That map was fetched here. Now, 'tis one or the other of you has it—you or the boy."

"Leave me fetch the brat downstairs, 'Lishe," grumbled Prettijohn judiciously.

"Tut, Master Prettijohn," said Elisha. "I reckon he'll come on his own legs running when he hears such sounds as this little doxy will be making presently."

"Dan knows nothing," Sally cried. "He didn't see the map."

"Hah, the dousing rod bends!" cried the dwarf. "The map then. What place did it point to? What place, I want to know!"

"I—I don't know."

"You were there!"

"I'm blind!"

"Then you heard them say!"

"I can't remember."

"More's the pity. I've marvelous good means to sharpen recollection!"

I strained my cheek to the thin panel till I wonder the wood did not creak. I was numb with desperation and had my finger already in the small copper ring which would slide the panel soundlessly open. I might have been a match for one of them—even the dwarf, for I was fast—but the three of them were too much for me. Still I figured wildly to spring out and take them by surprise, snatch Sally's hand, and chance a scramble into the safe dark of the hall. If it came to a skirmish on the hearth I judged I would be quick enough to seize the hot poker from the coals and let the swiftest fend off. But something in me counselled that it was a time for wit, not wildness, and I had a clear, strong hunch that the moment for wit was almost nigh. But Elisha sprang suddenly close to Sally.

"Up, little missy," he cried. "If there's one thing eases a hard memory it's a soft seat."

And with that he seized Sally under the arms and carrying her to the board he set her upon the chest of the dead man.

"Tut, now! Why d'ye shiver so? Is there a draft? Ain't

there fire enough in the chimney? And why do you hunch away from touching? I'll wager your feather tick is hard by comparison. That thing you sit on ain't hard—it never was hard, though it fancied itself to be! Tell me now. Don't such a high, elegant perch improve your recollection about maps and such, Lady Lamps-out?"

Sally's hands stole dreadingly round her, feeling the worn tow shirt, the buttons, the open collar, her fingertips recoiling when they brushed by chance the loose-lolling chin.

"It's—cold," she whispered, almost choking.

"Ay, it's cold as Death, for Death it is. And ain't Death-at-Hand another real good memory sharpener, missy?"

Hard cases as they were, it was plain that Blue and Prettijohn shared uneasinesses about such fancified extortions. And all throughout Elisha's awesome little performance Prettijohn kept up a mumbling underbreath recital of all the demons and misfortunes which might come tumbling soon upon them for the devilling of a blind girl.

"Ay, if Barnaby was here," muttered Blue suddenly, looking my way, and I thought he had spied my eye at the hole till I knew he was staring at the head on the stool. "Ay, if only he was here. How well I mind the nights when we'd wait to wreck the flatboats on the bar below the Devil's Elbow. It was clean as town shopkeeping then, Mister Prettijohn. No maps nor brats nor such murky trade as this. It was stand or stampede—it was case knife and pistol and make for the shoals as soon as we heard Barnaby's high sign from the bluff. Do ye mind that whistle of his, 'Lishe? Sharp as a redbird and 'twould carry a mile upwind! And then we'd wade out and wait for the flatters to ground on the shoal. That was thievin' like thievin' was meant to be. I tell you I don't like this game with blind eyes, 'Lishe! I said it once and I don't mind saying it again. It's like throwing ashes upwind!"

"Shut your damned mouth, Blue," muttered the dwarf, and waddled to the hearth and fetched the poker out and held it up till it seemed to scorch the corners of the shadows.

"Shut your damned mouths, the both of ye," he said, moving in on Sally with the poker held high and white-hot as a glowworm on a stick.

He lifted a curl of Sally's dark hair and draped it in the air for a second before he lifted the iron and burned it through with a hiss and wisp of drifting blue smoke.

"A gal may not miss her sight," said he. "But I'll wager that God's own wife would sing to save her *looks.*"

I saw Sally's nostrils quiver as she smelled the burning of her hair and her cheek flinched away from the feel of that heat so near and in the very moment before she gathered breath to scream I put both fingers to my teeth and gave a whistle that shook the windows. For a spell nobody moved and there was no sound but the drum of the flame in the chimney. Then Prettijohn swung his stricken eyes slow to the head of Barnaby while Blue crossed himself. Prettijohn nodded.

"Ay," he whispered. "His whistle. And the breath that made it—all the way from Hell. What was I just a-telling you, Mister Blue? We've roiled up matters here we didn't reckon on."

Elisha stamped round and flung the poker on the hearth with a great iron clatter. Then he glared at both men, though I could see that even he was shaken. Blue's face was drained to the hue of white chicken gravy and Prettijohn groped for the bench.

" 'Twas that boy," whispered Elisha.

" 'Twas Barnaby," Prettijohn muttered in a croaking voice and, fetching a demijohn of brandy from the board by dead Turk's elbow, he ringed it up on his arm, gulping his dram raw from the stone throat of it and dribbling more all down across his shirt.

"You tarnal fools!" cried the dwarf. "I tell you it was that boy. He's out yonder in the hall behind that door."

But he still didn't make a move to see.

"That was no boy," Blue said, borrowing the jug from Prettijohn. "That was Barnaby Thorn's signal. Didn't I hear it come a-blowing up through many's the spring fog of a river night?"

"Ay, 'twas his all right," Prettijohn said. " 'Tis his way of scorning this business with the blind gal. I warned of it, 'Lishe, I did now."

"I'd know that whistle if I heard it in my grave," Blue added. "And, be God, I'd set up sharp—coffin lid or not."

"You fools, it was the boy!" Elisha screamed again before he scampered for the door, but before he went he fetched Barnaby's dried head a good long stare and I felt real complimented to have pulled off such smart mimicry, though I knew it was pure guessing and hunch and luck that made me chance it at all.

Sally's scared face took on fresh color then and I reckon it was knowing it was me close by somewhere as much as Elisha's laying off of her that plucked her up that way. Elisha's short boot kicked the door booming wide and I heard his short legs strut out into the blackness of the hall and go pacing up and down, poking at shadows and cussing until he struck a light.

"Boy!" he bawled. "You're somewhere nigh—I know that! Boy!"

Prettijohn and Blue both had faces that looked like a riverboat's mainsail when the wind was wrong; they both sat with their wrists between their knees and staring at the poor, dumb, dead, rain-weathered leathery thing on the stool, though I'll wager its complexion wasn't as sick and played out as their own.

Yonder I could hear Elisha striding up and down in the hall bawling after me in a great temper and I hunkered down there in my space between the thick walnut walls praying he'd not guess that such thickness might just serve to hide a boy. He was back in possession of his senses though and certain that the whistle had been mine and the thought that I had made it and yet remained somehow invisible had set him off into an awful frenzy of rage, and directly he was hollering after Blue and Prettijohn to fetch lanterns and come help him seek me out in the upstairs where he fancied I was hid.

It was half orneriness in me and half the notion that Blue and Prettijohn needed some little extra nudge to set them in motion that made me whistle again. I didn't do it sharp and loud with my fingers this time but kind of lowing, something like the soft, long hoot of a great horned owl, the way it will do sometimes in the dark of a cloud-cursed August night; it was a sort of little masterpiece of a whistle, low and lorn and lonesome, and I reckon the hollowness of those old, dry panelled walls gave it a kind of extra fiddle-box ring that helped ease it under their hides a little more. Blue sobbed like a boy and Prettijohn's lifted jug fell smashing between his boots and then both men flung scrambling and cursing through the open doorway.

It's downright queer: after all the mischief that had been out there in that room that night the thing I dreaded most now was slipping out that panel and going past Barnaby's head. Still I did it, though it seemed that I felt its hollow stare upon my back as twitchingly fearful as the thought that, at any moment, the reality of Elisha and the other two might presently come raging through the door again.

"Sally?"

"Dan. Oh, Dan'l! What'll we do!"

She sobbed the words and slid down into my arms and flung a hug round my neck that took my breath. I could still smell the burned-hair smell plain and it seemed to remind me all the more of how we need hasten. For it wouldn't take them long to find out that I was not upstairs and that would bring them back in doubled fury.

And yet I paused at the notion of dragging Sally into that yawning dark hallway to make the big break for the pantry door and the stables beyond, for there was a good chance that Barbara was yonder, biding her time to seize us both. I glanced quickly down at the open panel through which I had come. I hesitated. And in that twinkling the whole game was nearly lost. The sound behind me was so faint that I imagined—as if there had not been enough horror—that dead Jacob Turk had stirred stiffly in some broken-necked dream and dislodged the Indian penny from his other staring eye.

Then I whirled and saw him. He was one of those drunken, faceless shadows who had slept slumped throughout it all and yet now had risen and stood staring greedily at us both from behind the board. He was the one I think I had heard Prettijohn address as Sawney, and he was, indeed, a sandy-haired man with a flat nose and a scar, pale as a fishgut, that twained his face from forehead to chin, like a portrait sliced in half and shifted on its easel.

"You, boy," he whispered thickly. "Why, you're the one they're a-hollering after up yonder. 'Y God now, this is a smart turn of fortune. 'Lishe, he'll reward me good if I was to fetch ye to him!"

I started toward the yawning panel door, thrusting Sally's shoulders down before me.

"Naw, halt there, boy," snarled Sawney, fetching something bright from his pocket and prying it open. "Halt there now. Stand, I say! Move that one more inch and you're deader'n Cain's brother! 'Lishe, he said nary word about taking you live!"

He was drunk but not that drunk, having slept off the thick edge of it, and he stood now swaying lightly and leaning into his dirty fist on the board whilst, with the other upraised hand, he bounced the case knife on his horny palm like some useful, easy toy. I sucked in breath and chanced it. I fell upon Sally and the bright knife flew like a bird.

When I heard the thick whack of it and felt the sting and the gathering of the shoulder of my coat I was sure he had hit me. And I heard him come stumbling and clattering round the board and move cursing toward me. I pushed Sally on in and tried to follow but I was caught, the thick shoulder of my woolsey coat nailed by the knife to the wall.

"Damn ye, if I was sober you'd have felt hot blood," muttered Sawney and fell half upon me, seizing me by the other sleeve. Sally went scuttling on ahead—she, at least, was safe—as I struggled and he lunged his full weight down across me and I could feel his grog-soured breath like steam against my neck. But he was drunk and I was young and lively as a fish and before he could grab fair hold of me I had skinned out of my coat and left it behind, like a toad in spring, and went scrambling down the dark way after

Sally and hearing him as he went bawling off after Elisha through the halls.

The walled garden was empty, hushed—all white and blue with shadows from the veriest thin blade of moon that pried up the dark edge of sky beyond the apple tree.

I almost burst out crying with the relief of being so near safety but I knew there was danger in that lulling sense. The big stone stable beyond the garden loomed up in violet outline against the glittering sky.

"Come come come," I gasped. "Oh, Sally, be quick."

"Dan, I don't think I can go on," she sobbed.

"Hang onto me then," said I. "We'll make it. Once we get on old Peg's back we're as good as at the Major's."

Peg was Sally's horse—a fine old blazed-face Percheron who knew the way and had taken Sally there a thousand times without me. The stable was dark as the inside of a whale's belly and full of the good, bright, yellow ammoniac smell which seemed to me just then the very breath of salvation. I helped Sally onto Peg's bare back and led the old horse into the pale magenta moonlight of the cobbled yard. I gave one last swift glance at the open gate to the garden and saw the faint red wash of a swinging lantern's light among the frozen rose bushes as Prettijohn and the dwarf came flying in pursuit.

Things happened then so fast that I can scarcely recount them. Even as I swung one leg over Peg's back to mount behind Sally I saw the black looming shape and heard the striking hooves as black stallion and rider came out of the stable like a shot.

"Climb on, boy!" I heard Barbara shout.

And before she could speak again I struck Peg's rump a mighty smack and watched her go lumbering away with Sally.

"I say climb up, boy! You're dead if you tarry!" she cried again and something burned orange in the shadows by the garden gate and I heard the bang of a pistol.

"But Sally—!" I gasped, bewildered which way to go now.

"She's off and away!" Barbara cried. "Climb up. For God's sake, quick!"

She swung down and gave me a strong boost aboard and we fairly rode them down—Elisha, Sawney, Prettijohn, and Blue—and I hugged close to Barbara as we went down the steep drifts of the meadow and across the banks and the river road and made for the vast river ice. I heard shots yet behind us.

"Sally!" I sobbed into the wind.

"Devil take Sally!" shouted Barbara. "She'll make it to your damned Englishman. Devil take her, I say! It's us they're shooting at, boy!"

The pistol fire kept on behind us and the balls went singing through the air all round us like thick-winged hornets, but in a measure of moments we were clear.

"Where are we going?" I cried.

But she didn't bother to answer and the wind whistled round us and the hooves of the black horse rolled like a drummer on the thick ice of the great river.

When it seemed at last certain we had lost them we stopped in the great frozen shadow of a vast, ancient willow and Barbara cast me back a look.

"You lost your coat," she laughed.

I made no answer. I had indeed lost my coat and I knew suddenly how much more I had lost than a coat. But I said no more just then. Because the more which I might have said might have woken in Barbara a fury worse than Eli-

sha's. I kept shut-mouthed for the next hour as we rode
leisurely on downriver.

"You lost your coat," Barbara said again after a spell and
fetched a rough blue blanket out of her roll and told me to
wrap in it. She kept eyeing me in the dim moonshine as if
she figured me to break for it again. But I was done with
running for a spell.

I kept watching her queerly because there was no show
of pistol now and she gave me a sip of something burning
from her saddle flask. She seemed almost kind. And I didn't
trust that. And I sure said nothing about the coat, though
coat was all that filled my thoughts just now. I had lost my
coat to save my skin—and Sally's—and only Heaven knew
what fresh furies I need face because of that.

Because that old woolsey coat had pockets.

And in one of them was stuck the Major's map.

⁓⟨ 7 ⟩⁓

THE cold was like a thick, vast sleep.

She had built us a good little fire way back up in a steep-banked creek holler a full mile back from the river. She said when Elisha came downriver hunting us they wouldn't likely find us there. Since we had gone on wind-blown ice almost all the way there wouldn't be much tracks for them to follow. For a girl she seemed to figure out such matters pretty well. We heard a wolf snuffling round in the laurel and scrub pines once or twice but I reckon he wasn't after us because we heard him moon-calling half an hour later and it sounded a couple of miles off.

Barbara had herself a real good snort from the saddle flask and then just sat there a long, silent while, hugging her knees and staring into the flames with a pleased expression printed all over her face. After a spell she fetched out a little steel mirror in a pinchbeck frame like Gypsies peddle on the river road and studied her face in the fireshine. Cold as it was she bared her neck and looked that over for a little bit. Then she smiled and slapped her leg.

"I can sure see them pearls," she said. "I can just see them like they was dug up already. See them a-shining!"

I just sat there barefaced, not knowing when to spring it on her about the map and wondering where I could run to when she found out.

"They ain't dug up yet," said I.

But she just put her little looking glass away and bundled up again and went on smiling in the fire.

"They will be," said she. "We'll give 'Lishe and his boldy boys a chance to run their legs ragged and when they've plumb give up then we'll go treasure hunting."

"Yes'm," said I.

"You don't trust me worth a damn," she said directly. "Do ye, boy?"

I kept still.

"Well, you should," said she. "I did save your skin. And I let your little gal get away back there."

"Yes'm."

"I reckon you know what would have become of the both of ye if that damned 'Lishe had grabbed you."

"Yes'm. I thank you kindly, ma'am."

I cleared my throat.

"Still and all," said I. "It wasn't just a kindness. You're after me for something."

"I am," said she. "And it's as good as mine."

I kept mum for a long while then. I didn't trust her, like she said. Still it wasn't the way she thought. The plain fact of it was I never had put much trust in womenfolks of any breed, shape, nor form. Not even Sally. And I didn't trust Barbara for some of the same reasons. It wasn't just because she had come after me with a pistol there in the attic, it

wasn't even because she had kidnapped me for the secret to
the treasure. The things I didn't trust about Barbara were
some of the things I had begun to feel lately in Sally: a sort
of softness and wishy-washiness you couldn't really count
on. Sally had changed a good bit in the last year or so and it
was purely a change for worse, a change toward a certain
something I could sense even stronger in this female, Barbara. Still I found myself missing Sally something fierce
right about then and I kept worrying about her making it
to the Major's safe. While I was thinking all this Barbara
was watching me close.

"Well, Merry Christmas, Dan'l Cresap."

"Merry Christmas, ma'am."

She stared at me a spell more.

"Did you ever get a Christmas gift, Dan?"

I studied that one over for a bit, then blushed. "Yes'm."

"Just one?"

"Yes'm."

"I bet it was from that gal," said she.

I kept mum, redder than ever and hoping she'd figure
my blushes was firelight.

"Was it a present from her?" said she.

"Yes'm," said I with a testy sigh.

I never did see such a female for questions, I thought to
myself. I half wish she'd go after me about the map.

"What kind of present was it?" she asked.

"Oh, just some little old thing," said I.

One thing I liked about Barbara was she could cuss like a
drover when she got worked up to something. She kept on
about me telling her what it was Sally had given me because she said she'd never gotten a Christmas present in her
whole life. I just sat there getting sweatier by the minute
because she wouldn't let up till I gave in. Directly I opened

my shirt and pulled the fool thing out and handed it to her.

It seemed a silly thing to treasure and a sillier thing to show but Sally put a lot of store in it and made me swear in blood to wear it always. The summer before there had come wandering up river an old Acadian from the Bayou Teche country in a broken-down pirogue who painted little portraits on pieces of ivory for a living. He did Sally's likeness—true to life but no bigger than the queen's head on an old shilling—and she had dug ginseng all year to pay for it and saved it by till Christmas to give me. The locket was genuine brass and the string was only a circlet of fishline but I wore it even if it did make a green stain on my chest. Sally put big store in my wearing it, even when I was sleeping, and to tell the truth it was a kind of comfort, in a way, since she was all I had, even if she was becoming stranger and more distant with every passing day. And I had to grant that the little face was the very living image of Sally's pretty face.

Barbara studied it a great long while and then gave it back to me.

"There's the gal you'll wed," said she firmly but with a wild, crazy flash in her eye like a Gypsy auguring the future from pictures in the fire.

I took that prediction mum, too, though I tell you the thought of it made me shudder and I kept on staring at Barbara, trying to puzzle her out. I didn't trust her but still she was a riddle that held my fancy fast. The way she cussed and rode and wore a dirk and pistol would match any man and I judged she'd be a fair hellcat in a fight. But still there was that contrary softness showing all over her and she had that sweet, silly, girl smell like Sally.

"Why didn't you leave me to Elisha?" I said suddenly.

"Because I don't hold with bullying children!" she said, almost shouting it.

She glared at me through the firelight. "Though don't never think I haven't taken sword and pistol to their daddies many's the time!"

She glared at me some more. "You figure I'm soft-hearted, don't ye, boy?"

She got up and strode round in the space by the fire, kicking sticks and leaves where the snow was melted and the ground shone through. She glared round at the tall, still forest night.

"I was her age once," said she. "And I was your age, too. And I had a brother your age named Johnny. You favor him in some ways."

The moon sailed free of a frost cloud and a few white flakes drifted past her face. She struck them off the tip of her nose and cussed in a grand, soft murmur.

"One night the savages came," she said. "And they drove us out in the snow and put torches to the cabin. Then they shot my ma and pap and granny. And they shot my brother Johnny, too."

She flung me a quick glance. "I tell you there's ways in which you sure favor him!" she cried.

She was still a spell then with her chin on her chest like she was trying to hold something in.

"Then—Why, then they scalped the whole family," she said. "Every last one except me."

I gave a big sigh of sympathy.

"Was they Delawares or Mingoes?" I said.

"What are you talking about!"

"Was they Shawnees? What breed of injun was they?"

"Injun!" she hollered, pitching a rock in the fire till the sparks swam up like a drove of fireflies. "Injuns! Hell, boy, *we* was the injuns. The savages that killed us—they was white Christians! Injun! God's blood, Dan Cresap, I'm half injun! But them hell-hearted sons of Satan—Girty and Greathouse—that murdered and scalped my family—they was white Christians!"

She stood glaring at me with her fists knotted white till I thought she was fixing to leap through the flames and throttle me. Then the anger seemed to pass off as swift as a cloud across the moon and she sat down again, chewing moodily on a sassafras twig, her gaze lost in the fire.

"That gal in the picture," she said. "The little blind gal, Dan. She's the one you'll wed."

It was so quiet beyond the halo of the fireshine that you could almost hear the brown bear turn and stir in his suck-pawed winter dreams.

Then Barbara slapped her hip sharply like she wanted to dispel all memories of her gloomy recital.

"Yes, you'll wed her, Dan," she cried. "And with all that gold that'll be your share of the treasure—why, you'll be the best provider in the whole of the old Thirteen!"

She folded her arms and smiled down at me.

"Now let's see the map," said she.

I tried to make a bold face of it. I sat there staring into the fire and trying not to blink till my eyes watered and a great lump lifted in my throat. Then I started in to cry right off. It had been a right good spell since I'd ever cried about anything excepting Pap's death and that wasn't as hard as this somehow; it was like the breaking up of river ice in the spring thaw and nothing to hold it back. It was hopeless to try to hold it back and it was ecstasy to get it off my chest and I told her most everything—about how I'd lost the map when I skinned out of my greatcoat getting away from Sawney's hands and the next thing you know I was even telling her about the poor Frenchman and how he'd fetched me Pap's little chest with its three clues—even if I didn't name them—and next thing I knew I was telling her the part about the map's being a counterfeit just to lead other hunters on a fools' chase so's me and Sally and the Major could go after the treasure in a genuine, proper way. I don't know what had seized hold of me—it was like the fever or an ague and it seemed like once I'd said the first word there was no holding my tongue. It was all so foolhardy, I know, but—well, it's nigh impossible to tell a lie or keep a secret over a campfire. So I even ended up promising to cut her in. And when I got done I felt marvelous calmed down. It seemed like I'd been holding something back for years that had wanted telling to a woman.

I was dumbfounded how easy she took it. Directly she had her arm around me and was hugging me tight, but it was all right because she done it in a real chummy and boylike way.

Directly she gave me a sad, twisted grin.

"I thank ye, Dan Cresap," she said. "We're sworn friends for life."

And we shook on it, like men, and I felt better than I had in years.

"Still, maybe your Englishman won't want a lady bandit for pardner," said she presently. "And your little sweetheart—she'll be jealous."

"It's my treasure," said I. "And I'll share it as I please. Besides, Sally, she's been taking a whole lot too much for granted here of late. Anyhow—four ways is better than three—it's squarer. And you been square with me, Barb'ry."

"Well," said she. "We'll have to move easy. You can bet we're being hunted at this very minute. I'll vow 'Lishe and those cutthroats are watching the river road tonight."

Then she went and fetched the horse and flung the saddlebags aboard and told me to help her while she commenced throwing snow on the fire.

"We'll hide out all this Christmas Day," she said. "We can stay aboard a boat I know that's froze up for the winter downriver a piece."

The fire was smothered by now and where it had been rose a mound of gray, melting snow with steam curling up from it against the twist of new moon.

"Does your English Major think he knows where the treasure's really hid?" she said.

"I'm sure of it," said I. "He's smart as paint."

"Has he got the three clues?"

"All except one," said I. "He let me keep one. But he's seen them all three and pondered them good and studied them all over. He's got it all figured out what they mean by now, I judge."

"Which clue have you got?"

And I dug into my pocket and showed her the strange silver ring with the Gorgon's mask on it, all grimacy and fierce with its tongue stuck out and savage eyes a-glaring there in the moonlight. The Major had said I could keep it till we went to hunt the treasure because I'd wanted to bear a talisman of some kind to remind me of poor dead Pap.

"And they'd need that ring to figure out what the other two clues mean?" said she.

"Yes'm."

"So that even if they found it on you—it wouldn't do them any good without the others."

"Yes'm."

"Then, Lord's sake, don't lose it," she said, swinging

aboard the horse and fetching me a hand to follow behind. "Don't let it joggle out of your pocket as we ride."

"I won't," said I. "How far are we riding?"

"An hour," said she. "Maybe longer since we have to stay back from the river. But hang on, Dan—I'll get you there sound and solid."

We followed an old Shawnee trail she knew among the drift and twist of those tricky hills and a couple of times we nigh bogged down in drifts but the horse kicked free and bore us, at last, out onto a ridge above a clear white slope of bottomland pasture that fell softly to the frozen river's rim. The willows were thick and snowbound on the shores but deep among them I spied the red smear of a lantern in a frosted window and heard the thin, brassy twang of a banjo. We approached cautiously; Barbara had her pistol out and cocked and was eyeing the white distances to North and South with an expert roadman's eye.

When we drew close I saw it was a high-masted house-boat of some sort: a great, squat business, nearly long as a ropewalk, and it was tied in at shore among the cold willows, though it didn't need any cord to keep it there, being as it was gripped helpless in the vast sheet of frozen river like a nut in the icing of a cake. From a good-sized chimney pipe in the flat, sloping roof smoke curled out among the willows in the moon like a sleave of ragged yarn strung loose upon the starry sky.

"Now mind ye," Barbara said, tying the horse to a young elm. "Keep mum and look dumb and let me do all the talking. Don't breathe a word about treasure. This is the keel-boat of Doctor Longo and he's a little strange, I fear."

"Does he know you?"

"Ay," she said, with a wry smile. "We've met."

"Is he kindly turned?"

"He's as good a friend as any," said she. "So long as there's no gold comes between. And another thing, Dan'l—"

"Yes'm?"

"Don't panic and bolt when you first step inside," she said. " 'Tis an uncommon strange establishment he keeps."

So we knocked and waited and knocked again and waited some more and directly the banjo quit and we heard light footfalls on the door's other side and a man's slow breathing at the crack. Barbara knocked again, sharp this time, with the pistol butt, and said her name plain.

"Is 'Lishe with ye?" asked the voice of him we'd heard breathing.

"No," she called. "Me and a friend, Jeremy."

There was a lot of sharp clattering: he must have had a half dozen locks and latches to undo, but in a minute the door swung open on a cheery big room with a fireplace and table and chairs and a general air of genteel comfort. The host bowed to Barbara like a gentleman of tone while I studied him.

"Who's this lad, Barb'ry?" said he in a high, pleasant, cheerful voice. "Who's this likely-looking boy?"

"Name's Dan'l," she said.

She gave a laugh. "I'm tutoring him to the trade," says she.

"To which fine aspect of the trade?" cries he, with a twinkle. "To robbing on the pike? To scuttling flatboats? To letting a little light into the skulls of dark-minded and unreasonable travellers? Hah. He does look like a likely lad at that, Barb'ry!—A bright-eyed eager boy, I'll wager. Are ye bright, boy? Do ye learn fast? Good. I can see you do! Maybe in a day or two I can teach you a thing or two, eh? Would ye be grateful for that, boy?—Lessons from the master hand of Doctor Longo himself! Would ye like to learn a thing or two, boy?"

"Such as which, sir?"

"Why, such as this!" cried he. "My my! We mustn't be careless, boy. Isn't that the first sterling lesson Life must teach us? For how can we learn to take till we've learned to keep?"

And beneath my boggling stare he held up his hand and from his thin, swift fingers dangled the circlet of string with the locket of Sally's portrait on it. My hands flew to my neck and, indeed, it was gone.

Barbara chuckled, watching, while I stood gawping as he hung the string ceremoniously round my head again and even tucked the locket in the open neck of my collar and gave my chest a pat to shake it down in place. He stood with his head thrown back and tilted, scowling at me speculatively.

"As for the other," said he, philosophically. " 'Tis a curio but I wouldn't dream of keeping it. The locket was brass and that's bad enough. But silver is worth little more. I'm a gold-fancier through and through. Moreover, I make it a policy never to pick the pockets of boys. Fishhooks, sir. Fishhooks and toads. But I see you carry no fishhooks, boy, nor toads either. Ah, but 'tis winter, that's why. Still—winter or summer—you *are* a careless boy. You must surmount that weakness, sir. Careless boys are poor pupils in the trade I teach. D'ye see, boy?"

He opened his hand again and now upon his pale, broad palm staring at me, as it were, with a grimace twice as derisive, was the silver ring of Pap's three clues. I shot a quick glance at Barbara, who had sobered quickly at that, and I bowed my head so he might not read my face as he dropped the ring carelessly back in my pocket.

He was a small man but his swiftness somehow gave him the effect of height. He had sharp blue eyes, cold as river ice, and black moustaches like a Gypsy bear trainer, and wore a fine shirt of red and white calico and over that a coat of good green velvet and high, tight britches of black woolsey with a broad calfskin belt with a bright yellow buckle and a watchchain of thick-linked gold.

"And where's 'Lishe, Barb'ry? Not hanged, I hope?"

"Not yet," said she.

"Is he out of Nashville jail yet?"

"Ay, last fall. He cut his way through the logs and rode off on the jailer's own mule."

"And the fine lad here—has he joined the gang?"

"I've quit the gang, Jeremy. This boy is a kin of mine. We were travelling north to Wheeling and felt the loneliness of Christmas Eve on the river road and not a tavern for miles. I reckoned you would bed and board us for the day."

"Ay, Barb'ry, to be sure! Chumship is a lifetime thing with me. And I'll not soon forget that ill-favored night two summers past when you and 'Lishe saved me from the mob that meant to drown me off the wharfboat at Shawneetown! Meanwhile—though he is, indeed, a most careless lad—maybe I can teach this fine boy at least to turn up watches. Purses—that's another matter. We always start with watches, eh, lad? A dip and a flip and snip off amidst the crowd. Barb'ry, didn't I always claim that one quick boy was worth any two men if he knows the business. Boldness! The boldness of youth! That's what I like about boys. A man will think twice and hang back betimes—but a smart boy will think three times and clip the boodle while a man's still pondering caution. Thought!—'Tis a tricky and dangerous habit, boy. Did ye know that? Cleverness!— That's what counts. And a dram or two of boldness to lace it! Eh? What say, lad? You look both bold and clever. Would you like to learn the trade?"

He chucked my chin and patted my shoulder and clapped me on the head.

"No mind. No need to hurry into decisions. Look round a bit. Do ye like flowers, boy? Do ye like History? What's your fancy, lad? Villains or violets? Heroes or heliotrope? Blossoms or blackguards? Eh?"

He turned and swung his hand expansively round the room and for the first time I saw them: flowers, flowers, they were everywhere in profuse, nodding bouquets beneath small glass bells on carved cherrywood pedestals. I sniffed and smelled no smell but that which pervaded the place: the not unpleasant, thick odor of wax as it always smelled in the kitchen of the Golden Sickle on brisk autumn days when poor Meg had used to put up quince jelly and wild black-cherry conserves. Flowers in every corner and table of the room and yet there was no scent of them and Doctor Longo led me round and pointed them out with pride and explanations of vast botanical detail. For he was, indeed, an artist in wax and, I reckoned, when he was not busy stealing he was peddling his wax bouquets to the genteel parlors of Wheeling and Louisville.

"Delphinium Tricorne!" he cried, pointing to a delicate bunch of larkspur, and then moved on. "Gentiana Crinita! —The fringed gentian of field and meadow! But, tut! What am I thinking of? What boy gives a fig about flowers! That's nonsense! I wouldn't give you a plugged brass farthing for a boy who liked flowers! Posies is for gals, eh, boy? What boys likes is History! Eh? Don't you like History, boy? Come then, boy, and meet Doctor Longo's garden of the great!"

He led me to a door and seized up a lantern on his way

and dragged me by the hand across the threshold. And while I stood watching in the dark he lit a taper at the lantern's smoky throat and went ahead of me down the long dark echoing hallway of the vast room lighting candles as he went, like a necklace adding diamonds one by one. And as he went, figures sprang into shape on either side and I lifted my shaking hand to my eyes and swayed as if in some stunning dream. On every hand stood earth's every kind of man and all of them famous and some of them dreaded and each of them dead as old Adam—General Lafayette and President Washington and the murdered Chief Cornstalk and old George III as big as life and mad-eyed as an August dog; and mingled among them, as if in some mischievous caprice of Doctor Longo's wit, stood villains and rogues famed up and down the river lands from Pittsburgh to Poverty Point: the Harpe Brothers and old Mason and highwayman Hare and Simon Girty and bloody Greathouse, and, down at the farthest end on a gallows of real oak, Barnaby Thorn hanging in a noose of real hemp. And all of them wondrous and all of them watching and all of them as waxen as the flowers. The candles that stood in little shelfholders all the length of the long barge room cast shadows that set the eyes of all these creatures twinkling. And it seemed as I watched that their very features winked and grimaced and grinned.

I stood, still stunned, and staring with mouth agape like every country fool who came to see these wonders in the little towns and settlements along the river in the easy months of summer—who came and paid his dime, I thought to myself, and had his pocket eased of any other coins which might burden it.

"Come yonder, boy!" Doctor Longo was calling to me from the echoing deeps of the hall. "History! That's what boys want—not flowers! Come, boy. Here, here! Never mind the General from Williamsburg and that French fop in lace! Here—looky here! Here's a murderer hanging! And there—on your left—Marat bleeding in his bath. Careful!—Lord, I never saw such a careless lad! You nearly stepped on poor Master Raleigh's head where it has just this last unhappy moment tumbled from the headsman's block. What's your fancy, boy? Pistols or patriots? Highwaymen or huffing, puffing hypocrites? Come. Don't you want to see the hanging? Here! Haven't you ever woken in a dream of hemp? No, I'll wager not! You're too tender-aged for such introspections. You haven't killed your first man yet, have you, boy? No. Too young. Still—I was only twelve. Here. Come along. Let me show you this. D'ye know this fine fellow? Benedict Arnold in the very act of boarding the British frigate—"

He seemed quite beside himself with some fresh zest at having someone come in the dead of winter to see his wild gallery and I wandered like a sleepwalker amid dreams, though they were so real to me that I could fairly hear the breath of some of them as I passed and, it seemed, a faint whisper of others to come rescue them from where they stood poised and historied and frozen.

I was fascinated, I was held—and yet I felt a chilling reluctance to let that chamber envelop me too far. It seemed that if I went to the farthest end from whose shadow-dancing deeps Doctor Longo beckoned, exuberant and eager, hospitably sweating, I might somehow be imprisoned within a waxen dream of my own. So vivid and lively were these posed mannequins that it seemed almost as if such had been their fate: that they had been captured there by a trick, as if lured out of history—as though they themselves, like the gullible summer crowds who came to see them, had each once come meandering down that hall and by some awful spell of Doctor Longo had had the souls pickpocketed from them and then been trapped like gnats in amber for all time. I stood swaying a little, moving dreamily like someone underwater and letting my stunned eyes move round and among it all in careless random. Glass eye and periwig—beeswax and tint—brocade of kings and towcloth shirts of hanged men. I wandered off a little to one side and for a spell I was lost in that forest of hushed and staring authenticity. I lifted my eyes to a candle inches away from my face in its holder on the wall. I saw its tallow tears begin to drip and for an instant I was caught with a child's choking fancy that I myself was turned to wax and melting. I stumbled and turned and stared back, longing, toward the door through which I had come.

I did not know where Barbara was. I judged she had seen the show before and now had pulled her boots off and was toasting her feet at Doctor Longo's fire or was, perchance, warming her stomach with a nip from a demijohn of good Frankfort bourbon. I heard him call again and I felt ungrateful in the face of his enthusiasm. What's worse, I felt he would think me dull—and a terrible coward, to boot. I set my feet manfully toward the back of the chamber where I could see him sitting now, rather glumly and considerably subsided, at a small candlelit desk. I walked timidly over and stood before him. He sat there with his hand raised to his forehead, shading his eyes, and apparently reading a book. He was quite still, in the manner of someone who had been mightily offended, and I hardly knew how to begin.

"It's all very wonderful, sir," I said.

I stared at the top of his head which now, without his wig, was quite hairless. The very angle of that head and the moisture on the bald skin seemed hot with indignation.

"You mustn't be offended, Doctor Longo, sir," I said.

"I'm only a boy, sir, and I don't reckon, sir, I have the fine words as could let on how mighty elegant, sir, I think all this is, sir."

"You don't have to. You already have!" he said from behind me and laid his hand on my shoulder. "Tut, now. That *is* almost my masterpiece. Me by me. Tut, now, boy. Would you not call me, in the veriest sense of the word, a self-made man?"

To tell the truth I had almost fainted at his touch and his voice behind me and I stood there astounded a moment longer with my finger upraised to touch the cold, smooth wax of that hairless pate.

"Why, I manage some of my slickest dips when they're staring at me there. And why not, I say? It's sure they'd not know it was me who plucked their pretty feathers, eh!— Not if they've got their eyes on me all the while. Come now! Did you feel a thing, boy? Tell me on your oath. Did you feel the barest brush?"

"No, sir. But—"

"But nothing. You're a very careless boy. We must amend that. Very careless, indeed. For example, look to your britches there. 'Tis the dead of winter and far too chill a night to be so bare."

And at the very instant he handed me back my belt I felt my trousers fall down round my boots. He shook his head, studying me gravely, one finger set among his moustaches and alongside his cheek. I stood before him, shivering in my drawers.

"Indeed, I wonder now," said he, "whether we have here the honest makings of a thief, at all. D'ye wish to learn purse-craft, boy? Yes or no. It takes honest stuff, d'ye realize that? The thread of a first-rate rascal is like good cloth—it must hold in the warp and the woof when 'tis tugged. 'Tis every bit as sturdy as the stuff of an honest man. Did ye know that, boy? Too many scoundrels kick off from the scaffold because they're cheapjacks, sir, cheapjacks! A first-rate rogue rides scotfree—and goes in carriage!"

I could only gawp and nod and I had already begun to feel—as any boy would—a discomfort at this detection of my lamentable shortcomings in the matter of mischief. As it was I was having enough trouble tugging my trousers back up and getting my belt back in loops and properly buckled to make any promises of repentance.

"Tut, never mind!" he cried presently, blowing his nose on a bright taffeta kerchief. 'Tis Christmas Eve and no time for schooling. We'll swing round to such fit subjects in the morning. D'ye mind bunking here, boy? I'm reserving the guest cabin for the lady."

He pointed to a nice straw pallet against the rear wall, with an old apostle quilt and a tattered green horse blanket. It looked, if anything, fancier than my bedding in the garret of the Golden Sickle and I was dog-tired. The place I was to sleep was in the very rear of the hall, in a snug corner well away from the draft that whistled faintly round the cracks of the single window to starboard. The pallet was thrown, in fact, just behind the spidery little Williamsburg desk where sat the Doctor's image of himself, brow-shaded, in philosophic meditation. On the desk among the litter of foolscap, inkhorn, and quills stood a candle in a high, thick stick of burnished pewter and, between that and the Doctor's waxen brow, stood a jigamaree and upon its carved fruitwood pedestal rested its small, clear glass globe of water which focused some of the light on the Doctor's still hand and spread the rest round the floor in a pearly, shimmery halo. Doctor Longo had taken the lantern with him and gone off among his creatures, snuffing out candles as he went and nodding fancifully to his favorites as he passed them and seeming, as it were, more courteous to some than to others and muttering pleasantries to each. I heard him then show Barbara to some small cubby of dust and quilts apparently just off the main cabin. There were words exchanged which I could not distinguish, with Barbara's voice grown sharp, and then presently the sharp throwing of a bolt and I could hear him go grumbling back to his chair by the fireside where, I reckoned, he would sit out the night.

The whole boat was dead still now except for the faint moan of the wind outside and the whistle of it at the drafty window crack and some part of the boat out yonder which swung from the mast in the wind, creaking like a roasting jack. The very notion of sleep was beyond me just yet, there, between the pages of that gaudy history book. I fetched up the candle from the little desk, determined to prowl and poke around a bit, as if Life would ever give a poor boy another such chance to move so free and uncontrarily amid cutthroats and heroes and kings.

"A damned flirtigig," I heard Doctor Longo exclaim once or twice in the stillness of his cheery front room. "She's nought but a whiffling flibbertigibbet, that gal!"

I reckoned he was mad at Barbara for locking him out, but after a spell his lantern went out and I could hear him grumbling and crawling into his blankets before the hearth.

I thought suddenly of the silver ring in my pocket and felt for it anxiously. I stared at it in the soft candlelight and stuck my tongue out at its moonlike, grimacing face. I remembered how easily Doctor Longo's swift, educated fingers had fetched it out before and I determined right then on hiding it someplace until the morning when Barbara and I were ready to go. In no time at all I had chosen the very place—the fourth pocket down on George Washington's pale linen vest. I approached my hero timidly—it seemed to me as if I were plotting an impudence—and my hand shook as I pried the pocket open and dropped the ring inside and as I felt the vast body of soft cotton padding beneath the cloth I had a sudden terrible fleeting illusion that all great men were really stuffing underneath and that all great, brave faces were only wax for Time to melt. When the ring was safe I stood back, staring up respectfully, half inclined to bow and thank him for his kindness, and I even hesitated for a moment before dispelling the fancy of swearing him to secrecy. Still I couldn't just back away, some gesture was demanded, and I settled for a smart Continental salute like I reckoned poor Pap might have and for all I know did give him in those old, lost days of glory before Pap's backslidance.

Then I set about nosing around some more—poking and peering among that strange, silent assemblage. They seemed all waiting for something there—maybe the trump of doom, I thought to myself, for there was something edgy in the air of that chamber, which was not just the chill of the dark. My shadow followed as I dragged their shadows stretching in my candle's wake and I came to stand at last before the hanging scene of the devil whose head had stood on the pole near the Golden Sickle all those dreadful years and which now rested somewhere up the river night in Elisha's portmanteau. There was a fierce and awful calm to the scene—the hanging was done and the hangman in his black coat and black tricorne was standing back to watch in the midst of two or three of the Regulators with their fists and cudgels brandished in the air. And Barnaby in the rope. Perhaps it was some motion of the boat, locked there in its winter ice as it was, and though it could not have been that it seemed the coarse-cloaked, strangled figure swayed. But that was candlelight's trickery—I knew that with a sudden pleased feeling and I stepped back. And I stepped back slowly again and again. And suddenly I trod on a boot.

Then, as if in some gathering instinct of terror, I turned slowly and saw—not more than eight inches from my staring eyes—the leering face of the furious dwarf himself.

I did not scream but I did drop the light, pewter stick and all, and the tallow candle burned still in the dust on its side and it had dragged down all the shadows with it into shapes of monstrous and cocksure crookedness.

I stood staring, breathless, waiting for him to move. But he did not move, he had not even turned his face to see where I had turned to and directly I gave a great sigh and then a great laugh and fetched the candle tenderly up, nursing its flame, and fitted it back in its holder, and held it round on every side of that perhaps most marvelously lifelike of all the Doctor's images: Elisha himself. And I went presently back to my pallet, suddenly clean spent out and exhausted, and put the candle carefully back beyond the jigamaree at the Doctor's elbow and then went and sat a spell in the rustling straw of my bed staring across the room at the dwarf who did not even have the power to turn his fierce gaze to me. I got up presently and went through that watery halo of light the candle cast and snuffed it cheerfully enough. And the faint light from the cold curl of new moon flooded in faint from the quartered windows of that single starboard window. Elisha stood stiff and waxen in his square of blue dusk and yet so real that he still fair took my breath away. I laughed again and shut one eye and stared at him through the other, then shut the other and watched him with the left. The peace of Christmas seemed to clasp me at last and more it seemed than I had ever known it.

From time to time I woke from pleasant sleep and looked to be certain that he was still there—unreal but real as life, threatening but no threat: forever I felt beyond the terror of his wired, wax fingers' grasp. It was a zestful game and I suddenly loved Doctor Longo for having created it. He had made Elisha into a batting-stuffed dummy whose beeswax nose I could, at my whim, tweak and taunt.

I sadly noted as I crawled under my quilt that the Doctor had, for the second time, lifted Sally's picture locket—and this time he had kept it. But I pardoned him that, allowing he had spent a long, lonely, and probably unpurseful winter and needed this little picayune plunder to keep up his holiday spirits.

At least the silver ring was safe.

Even now General Washington was keeping it for me in his linen vest pocket, left side, fourth down, just past the twelfth horn button. It seemed, indeed, as if the tall, white-wigged Virginian stood staunchly there to guard me from the dwarf who, as I fell at last into deep, unvisioned sleep, glared off in moonlit impotence into the hushed, clothed garden of Doctor Longo's other marvelous dolls.

8

My restful, dreamless sleep seemed endless. And when dreams did come they were not nightmares, though the dream was nonetheless vivid. I dreamed I was in the pantry of the Golden Sickle staring at a great huckleberry pie that Suse had just taken out of the great brick oven and even as I stared at it there on the chopping table its crisp moon face of golden crust turned suddenly to silver and it had become the face of the Gorgon on the silver ring grown huge and as I watched it stuck out its tongue at me and on its tongue was a gold sovereign and it stopped grimacing so fiercely then and began to smile and more gold coins came popping out of its mouth. Sally was there and she and I fetched a silver knife and quickly cut the pie open and inside we found—not berries—but all of the treasure: pearl necklace and bars of bullion and enough gold coins to fill a wicker peach basket. And as we stood there marvelling and happy and wishing the Major could be there to share our happiness we heard the sound of the Major's two prize horses on the meadow outside and they were growing nearer—I could somehow always distinguish the sound of those high-bred East Virginia mares— and then we heard the ring of their hooves on the flagstones yonder in the garden. And I woke up—not, as I say, frightened but quivering in a tremendous state of excitement.

There was not a sound but the creak of a jib up above on the mast of the Doctor's boat and the dry, hissing sound of fresh snow flying again on the wind. I got out of my blankets into the chill of the room. And since I could tell by the window that the moon was gone again under snow clouds, I fetched a tinder and steel from my pants and struck a shower of sparks until the candlewick swelled once more into soft illumining flame. At once the shapes sprang back to life: towcloth and satin and shadow as I stood listening and staring by the little desk. There was no sound from the front cabin so I assumed that Doctor Longo still snored before his hearth and Barbara dreamed safe behind her bolted door.

The face of Elisha glared off in printed, waxen fury into space beyond my shoulder as I stole past him to the window and crouched by the sill. Again, I was not afraid, but somehow keenly aware that something was astir.

The thin line of ragged ridge trees showed black between the white vast expanse of rising meadow and the gray of the sky. The snow scratched thinly across it all till every shape of tree and bush behind it seemed scumbled and indistinguishable. Then suddenly in one vivid smear of orange I saw a lantern come wagging out from behind a tree and burn clear for a moment before it disappeared among boughs of rhododendron. I could not make out the shape nor face of the man who had held it, but in that

twinkling I did catch one clear glimpse of a horse's head and chest and I knew it instantly as Major Henthorn's piebald mare, Phoebus.

That had been the dream's reality. I had heard those hooves in my sleep, I reckon, and I reasoned that if the Major was out yonder on Phoebus then surely Wherry had ridden with him on Diana and they had come to fetch me home. For a moment I had a bright gala vision of us all having a great Christmas dinner at the Major's house that day: Sally and me and the Major and my new friend Barbara. I could hardly contain myself with excitement and wanted to run crying into the front cabin with the good news.

Then I remembered Doctor Longo. How could Barbara and I explain all this to him without letting slip the secret of the treasure? I was in a sweat at that thought, considering how much accounting for Barbara herself I had to make to the Major anyway. I knew at least that no word of treasure must dare be let slip near the ears of that seasoned old thief Doctor Longo or we would have another pardner on our hands and perhaps a dangerous one. Still, I knew I had to tip off Barbara as quickly as possible and I only hoped I could get her roused and past Doctor Longo and out the door before Major Henthorn, in mistaken zeal, stormed the boat to set me free.

The fire in the grate in the front cabin had nearly gone out. And the lantern was missing. Still, enough light shone to illumine the dusky tints of the pale wax flowers in their glass bells blooming along the shelved walls. And quite enough light for me to see the disorder of blankets on the floor and the empty pallet before the dying fire. Doctor Longo was gone.

The door stood ajar a few inches to let the gusty wind

blow its crystal dust of snow across the worn floorboards. I put my eye to the cold crack and stared out into the dark and saw a lantern again and this time made out the tall shape and the wide, thickset shoulders of a black-cloaked man whom I judged to be Wherry. For a moment I almost shouted. For it was plain that Doctor Longo had heard the travellers and, for all I knew, might now be out yonder cocking his long rifle to fire on my friends. I was in a great fuss over what to do. I glanced toward the bolted door behind which Barbara still slept. And just as I lifted my fingers to knock in soft urgency I started suddenly at some sharp, clear noise from deep in the rear of the gallery from which I had just come. The sound of something falling.

I went slowly to that doorway and peered inside. Nothing moved among that motley mob. The candle still burned at the spindly, oiled desk where Doctor Longo's image sat and the water globe of the jigamaree spilled a quivering circle of light across his waxen head and shoulders. Corday still poised, knife in hand, above dying Marat in his bath. The King of England glared out through the rope upon whose noose dangled Barnaby Thorn. Lafayette brooded in one shadow. Spy André skulked in another.

I crept slowly down the middle way. Something was amiss, a something changed that I could not see nor name. For a moment all the creatures there seemed come to life. A moment later—and even more dreadfully—only a few seemed alive and they watched stiffly among the different stiffness of the others. And as I moved, their eyes seemed to follow me and I knew not which was live face and which was waxen.

Then I heard the nervous, unmistakable whinny of the Major's Phoebus out yonder on the wind and all my pluck came back. The Major would turn up presently with Wherry. I would cover Barbara with a few careful words till we were away. She would help me make up some explanation to Doctor Longo and perhaps pay him a few shillings for the night's lodging. And then we'd be off back upriver to the Golden Sickle to start seeking the treasure in dead earnest.

Still I wondered what that sharp sound had been in the rear of Doctor Longo's gallery. Had something fallen? Of course! The window that I had left wide open had let in the wind and upset something yonder in the shadows. But I had not opened the window. I stared stupidly at the snow blowing lightly over Elisha's shoulder and tried to remember, tried to be sure. I felt a sudden choke of panic. But why? Soon all would be well; we'd all be on our way!

The window was open. I had not opened the window. Or had I? The panic rose thicker in my throat. I glanced quickly at Elisha. But he had not changed. For a moment it had seemed that it was his replica which had unnerved me. I stared at it, so near, so hateful, and yet so harmless. I moved toward it to shut the window behind, keeping that waxen face defiantly in my vision as I drew near. Suddenly I stopped. Surely it had been some trick of shadow and light, some quiver of candleshine through the jigamaree's globe. But I had seen it.

He had winked.

It was unmistakable.

The left eye had winked at me.

I shook my head and rubbed my eyes and stared again. And I saw the frills of the blouse stir upon that gross, broad chest in the rise and fall of its breathing. On the floor among the shadows under the window I saw the overturned dummy and knew that Elisha's knocking it there had been the noise I'd heard. Now he laughed. And the laugh was short and when it was out one hand flew up and seized my wrist in a grip like a rawhide thong. He drew me down until—bare inches from my eye—I felt the breath of his crooked, whispered snarl.

"Ay, now, Master Daniel Cresap!—We have little matters to sort through, you and me."

Up front I could hear men stomping snow from their boots and fetching wood upon the failing fire and the cheerful voice of Doctor Longo, who had doubtless gone out to welcome them in and was now learning the purpose of their visit. In a daze, in a dream, in a weltering madness of hope I kept listening, fancying that still I would presently hear among those awful sounds the hearty laugh of Major Henthorn and Wherry's nasal baritone. For even as the dwarf hauled me out into the room where stood Blue and Prettijohn and Sawney I wondered how—without violence to him or worse—the Major's prized mares had come into their hands.

"Where's that woman of mine!" roared Elisha. "Where's little Barb'ry? Fetch her to me, Jeremy."

I was tied now to a little straightbacked chair by the door and watched helpless as Barbara was dragged out and hauled up between Prettijohn and Blue.

"Ay, now!" cried the dwarf, strutting up to her. "Here's the little bird who thought to fancy her feathers with the prettiest plumes of all. And not so much as a pin feather for her beloved spouse. Eh, lady gay? Thought to have it all to yourself. Why, I knew your cut from the first! For when was there ever ary woman sheared from other cloth. Now then, chicky, since you've thrown in with this here cub Cresap you shall share his fine fate. And you know what my habit is with Cresaps. And when we've fetched up that treasure—why, dear Doctor Jeremy here shall have your cut. How's that fit your fancy?"

"You've not got hands on it yet!" she spat at him, struggling.

Elisha swung round to me then and came cockily over, smiling. He laid one big finger under my ear and gently traced a cold line with a broken fingernail across my throat to the other ear.

"I want to take my time with this one," said he. "That's not a meal to be gobbled. 'Twas his own pap that caused my brother's head to come to its present sad state as it lies in yonder box by the door. No, here's a feast of fury to be savored. But I've got other matters to attend to first. Jeremy—"

He turned to Doctor Longo.

"—Is there a room where these trussed birds can be flung till roasting time?"

Doctor Longo nodded and twisted his moustache and looked me over with a measuring, and not unadmiring, light in his eye.

" 'Y God now, 'Lishe," he exclaimed. "You tell me this boy has nigh got his fingers on a treasure. And to think I was wasting his time and talents with talk of schooling to pluck mere shillings from the camisoles and coattails of country jakes!"

"Why, let me school him for ye," said the dwarf, fetching out his case knife and warming the blade in the flame of the Doctor's lantern. "I'm a schoolmaster who's full of questions. We'll see if this boy has learnt his lessons."

"Hold off, 'Lishe!" Blue complained. "You said we'd leave business go for a few hours."

"Ay, 'Lishe," called Prettijohn over a tin cup of applejack. "It's been a long cold ride. Besides 'tis Christmas and you vowed we could frolic and booze a spell before we get down to hard matters."

" 'Tis fair, 'Lishe," cried Doctor Longo. "Besides, you've got to tickle my ears with all the facts about this treasure hunt. Throw these two in yonder stockroom, boys. They'll keep. Nothing spoils in this good winter weather."

The dwarf glared at me and Barbara some more but he seemed to be in what was, for him, a good mood now that it seemed he had the game fairly in his pocket, and they all kept clamoring at him to ease up a spell until he finally gave in, while they dragged me and Barbara off, trussed up, and shut the door upon us. Doctor Longo fetched a big square Wheeling nail and nailed the room shut and they all went roistering off then about the boat.

Barbara and I had been flung into a workroom of some description and lay on a floor amid shavings and dust and the smell of wax. We could hear them arguing now and then laughing and then singing a little and then arguing some more on the other side of the door, and it sounded like Doctor Longo had tapped a barrel of rye and I judged they were all on their way to another carousing party like they'd pitched in the common room at the tavern.

Enough light shot through the cracks and crannies in the board wall to show us the place we were at. In one way it was like a shambles after a fort massacre and in another it was like the ruins of some gigantic toyshop. Wigs stood about on easels like scalps; wax legs and arms and even hands lay propped and scattered round and limbless trunks leaned back against the walls like poor dismembered creatures awaiting the gathering up signal of Doomsday's horn. And here and there stood clusters of pallid, painted blossoms to lend the whole scene an air of scentless funereal elegance. I scooted my foot round till I could touch Barbara's boot with it.

"We're in the kettle now, Barbary."

"Ay," said she. "But the water's not boiling yet, laddy. So hold on and look for light under the lid."

I lay still, pondering a bit.

"Why didn't you try to throw back in with them, Barbary?" said I.

"Why, now wouldn't that have been a fool trick," she said in a soft voice.

"You might have saved your skin," said I.

"This pretty skin ain't lost yet, boy. Nor yours neither."

"Still, you could have said you was with him all along," I continued. "You could have said you was tricking me—and holding me till he got here."

"He'd not have believed it," she said.

"Maybe. You could have tried."

"By golly, now," she said. "You sure have got a poor notion of friendship, boy."

She thought on it for a spell more.

"Or is it just females you're set against?" she finished.

I kept mum at that and bit my lip because what she had said hit home. She didn't say anymore and the way she was quiet told me her feelings had been hurt.

"I reckon I still got some learning to do yet, Barbary," I said.

But she still kept quiet.

"I'm sorry," I said directly. "I take you for a friend now, Barbary. I meant no meanness in doubting."

"It's all right," she said directly. " 'Tis a tricksome world, Dan'l. 'Tis wise to go doubtful most of the time. Still 'tis a lonesome world, too—and we'd soon perish without a friend here and there along the way."

It's a strange fact that I wished Sally had also been there right then—in a way I felt I had something to ask her pardon for, too. I felt that if Barbara was all right to trust as a friend then I could trust her as a female as well, and if I could trust Barbara then I could trust Sally, too, and even be her friend in the very way I had grown afraid to be these last few months of her strange change. I was puzzled by these feelings and as if that puzzlement wasn't bad enough Barbara did a strange thing which made it, for the moment, even worse. She struggled herself around till she was just inches away from me, then she asked me to turn my face to her.

"I knowed your pap, Dan Cresap," she said gently. "He was a good man and I can see you're going to be a good man, too."

And before I had the chance to duck it, she leaned her face across and kissed me a good smack right on the mouth. I tell you it was a mighty strange place to get a first kiss and it left me quiet for a great long while, pondering. The odd thing was it didn't make me sore the way you might think it would. It just set me to thinking all that much harder how I could sort of take charge of things and rescue Barbara and me from that awful trap we were both in. I saw what looked to be a cobbler's knife a few yards off on a little footstool and I tried to make some progress toward it. But I didn't seem to be able to make much more than a few inches an hour, we were both tied up so good. Meanwhile we both listened to the commotion they were all making out yonder in the rest of the boat. It came and went in waves all that Christmas Day long and it sounded like they'd drink and sing and fight a spell and then fall still—maybe sleeping it off—and then rousè up and start in all over. It gave me the creeps. It gave me even worse feelings to imagine how they had come to get hold of the Major's two best horses. I wondered what else they might have laid hands on. Because the way they were acting it seemed like they were so sure of that treasure that, for the time being, they had forgotten all about us and were just abandoned to celebrating their good fortune. Once or twice I heard the ringing banjo and the twang of Prettijohn's Jew's harp among the thud of bootheels and for a spell there came the woody whine of Doctor Longo's fiddle—I knew it was he because it was the sort of tune he'd play: none of your "Nappy-cot and Petticoat" or "Billy in the Wildwoods" but a fast, mournful jig by Bach or some such dandified Frenchy.

Around dusk, which sets in early in those river winters, the whole boat fell silent and stayed that way till dark. I had reached my fingers to the little crescent-shaped cobbler's knife by that time and was trying to fetch the blade round to saw through Barbara's cords. When it seemed I was near success there suddenly came a great wooden outcry from the door. Someone had a mallet and wedge and was knocking loose the great nail in the jamb and in a moment the door flung wide.

Elisha stood there swaying. The room behind him was a pitiful sight, with booze shining round in pools and dirty mugs and broken-necked bottles standing upright on a pair of hogsheads by the door. It was the first time I had ever seen the dwarf tipsy and again I had that awful feeling that he would never have let himself get so if he were not sure he had the game as good as in his pocket. His clothes were mussed and untidy and his cocked hat on crooked and his black wig set awry. His face was fiendishly merry and ruddied by drink and the tilt of his tricorne gave him an expression somehow more raffish and peery. I fancied from the look of things that he had it in his mean mind to play games with us now and I hoped silently that it would be with me and not poor Barbara. My guess at his intentions proved correct. He pranced into the room, having caught sight of the little knife in my hand, and with his walking stick knocked it clattering from my grasp.

"Tut now, boy! Boys mustn't play with sharp-edged toys. That will never do!"

He bent above me and touched my forehead gravely with the cold steel ferrule of his stick.

"Besides," said he, "I have better games for you and me to play."

I was real proud of Barbara: she cussed Elisha something grand and struggled fierce as he seized me under the arms and hauled me off into the firelit room and set me upright in a chair near the radiant hearth.

"Tut, lady gay! Your turn will come. We have games for ladies, too. But first comes games for boys named Cresap!"

He slammed the door and fetched the mallet and nailed it shut again. Across the room in a corner Prettijohn snored in blankets like a foundered hound. In a split-bottom chair by the door to his waxworks chamber sat Doctor Longo, propped and motionless as his own painted image. The fiddle trailed from his fingers to the floor and from time to time he fetched up his other hand and, with his ear-finger, scratched his noddy chin. From the chamber beyond I could hear the nudge and turn of the other sleeping drunkards.

"Now then we get down to P's and Q's," said Elisha, facing me and looking like some mad, misshapen child in Doctor Longo's high-backed chair across the hearth from me. "First of all," said he, "let's see the map."

First he cut my bonds, and, though free to move, I dared not.

He reached behind the chair then and fetched it up and held it in the fireshine so's I could see the printed western Virginia counties like colored squares on a quilt and the mountains like a great worry-torn brow and the serpent of the winding river and the great cross and circle where the Major's pen had marked the spot to lead the rogues astray.

" 'Tis a fine treasure map," said the dwarf. "If the treasure to be sought is Hampshire apples and Augusta sheep. And looky, boy—'tis marked. What a sly mark, too. Moon Ripple—that's the mark. What a grand impressive mark to send some poor Tom-Noddy questing with mattock and spade. Dig here and I reckon ye'd find a catfish mebbe—or a river clam with mayhap a rude pearl. A grand treasure map!—Except that all but fools know that no rogue would bury treasure in a sandbar that lies half the year in a foot of shoalwater! Ay. The trouble with this treasure map is that 'tis no treasure map at all and there's no argument *hic* nor *hoc* about it. 'Twas meant as a fools' chart to send fools chasing and that's an end to't."

And he laid it gently and slyly on the fire and watched as the flame first blackened and then licked it up the chimney.

"We're a step nearer the truth now, boy? Eh? And a foot closer to the missing piece of the puzzle, eh? D'ye like this round of Christmas games I conjured up for ye? Now for a riddle. Boys all like riddles, that's well known. Now here's the riddle—Are ye ready?"

I said nothing, my eyes fixed on his bemused and half-mad face.

"What thing is square and covered with hair?" said he. "And as each can see is initialled J.C.? There's the riddle, boy. And here's the answer!"

And with that he reached round behind the chair again and this time fetched out the deerskin-covered chest that I had last seen on the Major's great table, among his maps and books. He sat a moment, fondling it and peering across the hobnail-lettered lid. Then he popped it open and fetched out first the spool of leadsman's twine and the scrap of almanack with Pap's poem. I stared in half-sick wonderment.

"Ho! The boy looks brighter now! I judge his wits are set working at last like good cider in the barrel. Did ye miss that riddle, boy? Then here's a whole passel of riddles to ponder."

And he waved the poem in the air for a moment before setting upon his nose a little, smeary pair of square-lensed spectacles, and began to read in a cracked, tipsy whine:

> Queen of Batavia, helter skelter
> Fled to Madeira's glassy shelter
> Gemini in Heaven point their light
> Heed not wrong but Hew to the Right
> Mark not the Phase which Only seems
> But under the sway of Pollux beams:
> Mexican cob and Spaniard's doubloon
> Lie hidden beneath the Full of the Moon
> There is no scoundrel still alive
> Knows these lie where the Hand is at Five.

"Tut, now," he cried, with a flourish of the paper. "That's plain enough. 'Twas meant for fools to think that the treasure was planted at Moon Ripple."

I sat half sick with dread. I had no thought of what he

was saying, of clues, of treasure, of hiding places, of anything save how this chest of things had come into his hands
and of what sad fortune had befallen those in whose hands
I had left them.

"What did you do to Major Henthorn!" I cried, squirm-
ing in my chair. "Where's Sally Cecil!"

"Tut, boy. What's all this whilly-wha? You're not even
listening. Here's myself who sit unravelling these great,
vast riddles right under your nose and you're not even
heeding me. Even though you'll not live to lay hands on so
much as a copper from that treasure chest, don't you want
to know where it's at? D'ye see. Under the moon! That's
clever, don't ye know. 'Twas under the Golden Sickle itself
that the poem means. The sickle—'tis the moon. D'ye see?
'Twas clever of your pap to fancify such ciphers. 'Tis pity
he has such a Tom-Noddy son!"

"What have you done with them?" I wailed. "How did
those things come into your hands?"

"Tut, boy. You ask too many questions. It's my turn
with a question. But first let me come round to it proper-
like. The poem says the treasure is buried somewhere
under the Golden Sickle. The Queen of Batavia who is fled
to Madeira's glassy shelter?—Why, that's plain enough!
'Tis to say the necklace is in a wine bottle snug in the chest
among the gold. But what's this pribble-prabble of Gemini
and Pollux! Why do these lie where the Hand is at Five?
There's only one answer to these questions, boy."

"Will you tell me at least that they're alive?" I sobbed.

"Ay. And I'll tell you more. But first you must give me
something."

"What do you want from me?"

"Why, the third clue," said he. "Any fool can see there's
a piece to this puzzle missing."

For an instant I almost gave in and told him of the ring that lay hidden in the vest pocket of George Washington in the very chamber behind the back of his great chair. But some last tinder spark of hope kindled in my brain that there might still be a long, last chance. Perhaps my fears about Major Henthorn and Sally were pure moonshine and those fears were driving me to give away the one clue that would give these rogues the game and maybe lose us all a treasure and our lives as well.

"Where's the third clue?" he whispered, grinning.

"I don't know what you mean."

"Ay, you know. And I could pry it out of you with the hot blade of yonder carving knife under your eyelids! I could do it that way but somehow this slow game is more fun. Where's the third clue, Cresap?"

"I don't know."

"And what is that clue?" he went on more hotly. "Is it a gentleman's pocketwatch? Is it a compass? Is it a sign scrawled scrimshawlike on a chip of ivory? Is it maybe a scarab?"

"I don't know what you're talking about."

"Ay, you know what I'm driving at and you know it well. 'Tis a small thing. 'Tis not in your pockets, for I searched you when I bound you. And the light fingers of Doctor Longo yonder—they would have had it out by now. Where is it, boy? The clues I hold say the treasure is buried somewhere beneath the Golden Sickle. The third clue—it points the exact spot. Where is it, boy?"

"I won't tell you."

"Ay, you'll tell me. Ay, you will. God help you, you will. For I've hardly begun my little list of surprises."

"Why should I tell you?"

"Why shouldn't you, then? For what good are pearls and

pieces of gold to a boy who is dead? As soon you shall be. As dead as them."

"It won't work!"

"Ay, as dead as them," he smiled again.

"As dead as—who?"

"Why, as dead as your great blustering Yorkshireman, that's who!" he cried. "Dead as that snivelling blind flirtigig! They went down in blood when we stormed the house."

"You're bluffing!"

"Am I, then? And if I was to prove it no bluff it will snap your wits wholly—I'm waiting on that. Ay, once you know that your friends are all gone you'll have no more stomach for this fox chase, I'll wager."

"I wouldn't believe you if you swore they were dead!"

"What if I was to *show* you, my little cub?"

And he reached round behind the chair again and fetched out a three-cornered hat that I knew on sight: a once good hat of London felt that now had a hole in the top and was dabbled over with a horrid dark stickiness, and he reached in back again and fetched out a sleeve that I knew, at once, to have come from Wherry's one good great-coat and it, too, was all gory and stained. I stared at a small blue feather stuck in the blood on Major Henthorn's hat and shook my head through my welling tears.

"It's a lie! It's a lie! That's the blood of a rooster. You stole those things and begored them. 'Tis a trick to make me tell!"

"And what of this?" he whispered, with the most awful expression I had ever seen on his face as he fetched out the portmanteau in which he carried Barnaby's head. He held it in his little lap and unsnapped the brass clasp. I stiffened as I always did before coming into the presence of that wizened, withered thing and I watched as the dwarf's hand hovered and paused above the open box before it reached in daintily and grasped the hair and slowly, smilingly, lifted the fresh thing out.

"What of *this,* little Cresap cub," he whispered again and fetched it up clear of the box. It stared at me with glazed, dead eyes.

The anguished, half-mad scream in my own throat seemed in that instant a sound far from me. I scarcely heard it, it was faint behind the thunder of my pulses; it was like a voice from my past, a sound that might have echoed all the way from the Golden Sickle so far away. And yet even as I fainted dead away my darkened vision held still the image that it had had so gruesomely printed upon it: the pale oval, the dark, familiar hair, the stained open lips, that poor ruined thing that Elisha had swung up so cruelly from the open portmanteau—the bleeding, fresh-severed head of Sally Cecil, her blind eyes staring in a blindness yet more profound than life's.

My swoon was deep but it did not last long enough. I would have wished it to last forever. In that moment I could have died and been thankful for the blessed surcease that dying was. There are peaks of anguish in life which establish themselves as peerless, like sharp ridges above a range, so that no pain nor sorrow that ever follows them seems anything but bathos and stale custom.

I opened my eyes at last, I stared dully at Elisha. It was all meaningless. He could do no more to me now. His plan of torture had been more exquisitely realized than if he had put hot knives beneath my lids or candles on my naked soles. Sally was dead. The words repeated themselves dumbly in my brain. And I realized in that moment how precious she had been to me and how little I had known it until now. I realized then and only then how deeply I had loved her whose poor axed head now rested nodding slightly on the hearth, its dead cheeks gilded and rouged by the cruel red flames of the logs.

Elisha's evil, dark eyes feasted as they fixed upon my grief and his twisted lip curled in a whispered curse of me and my dead pap.

"I pondered long and then I pondered it longer and then I pondered it a spell more," he whispered savagely. "I racked my wits and fancy to come up with the one thing to wound you worst, young Cresap!"

He fetched the awful portmanteau between his little legs again. He reached in again and this time drew out the withered head of Barnaby and I saw it without flinching and knew that it, at least, could never stir me to dread again—not after what I had just seen. It had shared room there in the box with Sally's head all the way from the awful scene at the Major's house, I judged, and I was thankful that she had been by then, at least, beyond the sensing of her fellow traveller on that ride.

"Here's vengeance sweet, Barnaby!" the dwarf whispered to the hairy, wizened thing on his knee. "Look yonder, Barnaby, to that boy's face. Ay, 'tis the very son of the one who led you into the Regulators' noose—damned Cresap. Ay, that's his spawn yonder. Can you see the boy's eyes yonder, poor Barnaby? Sweet vengeance, eh? Look ye, brother! Could hot flames from yonder hearth have ever struck from that cub's lips such groans of melancholy! No, I say. Look ye, brother! See how his face curls as the wit behind it crumbles. His mind is going, Barnaby. And he'll snap soon. Then the clue to the clue will come tumbling out."

Nor was he far from the truth. I felt a cold string of saliva on my chin from my slack, stricken lips and my eyes were dry from not blinking and my breath was a sick, dry whistle among my dry, bared teeth. I would have told Elisha the location of the Gorgon ring in a moment if he had chance to put the question to me again at that moment. But he was busy in his monologue with Barnaby's ear— coaxing his dead brother's eyes back so that they could witness my suffering.

My eyes fell numbly back again to Sally—to that last of Sally, to that little of her that I would ever look upon in this harsh life. And the tears rolled hotly down my cheeks as I saw a tear run thickly now down hers and I thought nothing odd of that, so near was my mind to madness. Elisha kept up his monologue with the thing on his knee, stroking its hair as if it were the head of someone who had come in just then from the sting of the cold night beyond and wanted comforting. And I kept on watching Sally's head there in the warmth of the fire, there on the hearth, and I thought how reasonable it was—so near was I to madness—that even as my cheeks slumped and sagged with sorrow so hers did likewise in sympathy, for it had always been thus in the stark, shared nursery of our lonely, common infancy, that we had each worn the other's grief like one sympathetic mask. So near was I to madness that it seemed no strange thing to me now that even as I watched poor Sally's left cheek—the one nearest the fire—it commenced to swell out queerly around the jaw, as if her mouth held within it a great damson plum from the poor late Major's orchard and nothing seemed amiss to me when the eye above it began to wink slowly, almost slyly—the lid creeping down and down until it had covered the eye and gone far beyond it in a dribbling clot of tears. What was she about to say? Her poor gaping lips began to tremble and droop. Was it her sorrow that she was about to express? I thought—so near was I to madness. Tears, tears, tears—the whole of her face was a-sweep with tears now until it all seemed melting like the moon behind rain clouds and through all these changes the features of cheek and lip and eye were puffing and twitching and then falling as if going through slow, successive phases of stunning emotions. She yawned.

Something stirred in my wits.

Something woke inside my wits, something still unruined and unmaddened woke and whispered in me. And when I heard that whisper of reason I snapped a look round at the sleeping face of Doctor Longo and I smiled.

Elisha was heedless of what was happening beside him on the hot hearth flags. He glared at me.

"Where's the other clue, Cresap cub?" he whispered in a hoarse, harsh breath.

I giggled like the madman I wanted him to think me—indeed, like the madman I had come so close to being.

"Where's the third clue, boy?"

I giggled again.

"Why, 'tis in the waistcoat pocket of Gen'l Washington," I cried in leerish, sidelong simper. "Gen'l Washington—dead four years this very month! Long live Gen'l Washington! God save the old Thirteen!"

Instantly the dwarf had sprung down to his legs and strutted across to me.

"I meant to pluck loose his reason," he muttered to himself. "But not to tip it into bedlam!"

He shook my shoulders and I let my head loll loose and laughed at him.

"Where's the clue, boy? Come round! Come round! Here, let me undo you. Here! Bide you still a moment!"

I shot a quick glance at Sally's waxy head. It had melted now till it showed only above the nose as if she were sinking slowly into a quicksand of hearthstone, and rivers of melting wax sputtered now and dripped down across the hearth and out onto the dry boards of the floor. Elisha undid me and slapped my face sharply from side to side.

"Where's the third clue, boy?" he bawled into my face.

"He's keeping it for me!" I crowed. "Our country's father—he's keeping it for me. Three cheers for Gen'l Washington. Hip hip—"

"Tut now! It's gone too far! This wants some antidote!"

"—Hooray!"

Doctor Longo roused at my shrill gay cry and rubbed his face. He stared about him boozily a spell and then his eyes grew sober with alarm as he saw what I was so carefully witnessing take place upon the floor. The wax of his afternoon's creation—the head of Sally that he had fashioned for Elisha from her likeness in the locket—it was nothing now but a wig—a wig in a pool of hot, smoking beeswax which spilled out and caught up in tiny flames among the hot coals of the fire and the flames licked fast across the boards and into the cracks where the wax had already flown.

"Alarum! Alarum!" bawled Doctor Longo in a hoarse falsetto, and fetching a blanket he began beating uselessly at the flaming wax which had spread and permeated flaming all down through the dry cracks and crevices below deck.

Elisha screamed and turned and in the profile of his face I saw fear for the first time since I had come to know that awful visage. There is one thing that each man fears in this world and with each man this thing is different and with this cruel, murderous dwarf that one thing was Fire. With another scream and no further look at me he had flung open the door and was gone into the snow.

The rest was like pieces of pictures on broken glass. The flames had soon spread everywhere. I tore my fingers open getting the great nail from the door behind which Barbara still lay bound. Drunken river pirates woke, rose, and came stumbling past me among the wreaths of choking smoke. I cut my hand on the cobbler's knife severing Barbara's thongs.

"Quick, Dan, quick! This way!" she screamed from the door that opened onto the fresh cold night.

"Wait for me!" I cried and dashed back, for the last time, into the chamber of Doctor Longo's doomed and motionless dolls. I ran up to General Washington. It was my fancy, I know, but it seemed as if the line of his stern mouth trembled in a smile. For a moment I hesitated before taking the liberty of picking my first and last pocket. When I had my ring again I stepped back and saluted smartly—the way I fancied my poor pap had done in a time as lost and gone as this one soon would be. I turned then and for a moment I was almost—by what I saw—enthralled beyond movement. The flames were at the ceiling now, flapping and blowing like yellow and vermilion flags, and everywhere and everything was lit and illumined in the wild, frozen pandemonium of that chamber. I knew that if I stayed many seconds more that I would not move again, that I would be fixed—if only by fascination—into the same stilted, doomed attitudes as theirs. Everywhere those famous faces drooped and grimaced and winked and leered and signalled to me—it was as though the heat had fetched them alive. Heads bowed, brows scowled, lips smirked, mouths yawned as if trying to speak—to utter, perhaps, the answer to some riddle that had long perplexed even me.

Kings nodded their heads onto the gallows-bound shoulders of robbers as if confiding something in their ears. Priests fell before dead queens. In the moment before I began to run toward the far dim door I caught them all in one picture, like a fast fanning shuffle of court cards. But they were all the same; they ran to earth as candles drip on pewter.

I stumbled through flames and smoke and melting flowers till I found Pap's box, the spool of twine, the poem.

Outside in the snow Barbara and I hid beneath old willows and among snow-heaped rhododendrons that clumped all round on the shore. We watched the river pirates scramble about on the ice, their drunken, furious, bewildered faces lit by the mighty flames.

Somewhere I heard a sound which might have been an animal—but it was the dwarf Elisha.

Somewhere else I heard another sound which might have been the hooves of fresh menace—but they were only the Indians, the ones Major Henthorn had welcomed to his family pew on Christmas Eve. They had trailed us there and were come to fetch us back to the Major and Wherry and Sally—who followed on borrowed horses close behind.

9

WITH that pack of rogues be-
hind us, rallying now for hot pursuit, there was no time to
spare even though we were all dead sober and they had
been, when last seen, stumbling and keeling from their
Christmas Day of rumbo and grog.

"Elisha, too, was drunk," I said.

"Ay," said the Major. "But I fancy his temper will sober
him as quick as will this icy wind the others. He's behind us
and you may count on it!"

We rode the river ice and the horses' hooves drummed
dully in the crackling stillness of the night. When we rode
in sight there was not lamp nor candle shining in any
window of the Golden Sickle. Its scissored black shape
loomed cold and empty against the pale blue dust of light
from the curl of new moon which stood in the once more
cloudless sky. The stars glittered so bright that they seemed
polished by the wind, though on the western hills lay fresh-
heaped clouds of new snows to come.

"Hold back! That's cat ice up ahead!" cried Wherry, as

our horses drew nigh to a gray, coffin-shaped area on the white expanse of frozen river. It was near the shore, under the very shadow of the great cold willow behind which, set into the steep riverbank, was the archway of red sandstone and the thick panelled oaken door which led into the old smuggler's tunnel back into the tavern's wine cellar. We halted our horses round the dark and somehow sinister oblong on the ice while Wherry explained.

"They done sawed a hole in the ice here," said he. "This river ice is nigh a foot thick but where it's frozen over at this point 'tis thin as glass. 'Tis cat ice, as I say, so don't let a horse set hoof upon it. For there's quarter less twain of water underneath and that would drown man and horse right quick."

"Why would they saw such a hole?" asked Sally, tilting her blind face in the moonlight.

I glanced quickly at the Major, who shook his head, and then he looked at Wherry and held a finger to his lips. And all of us save Sally looked down at what was most surely the cold grave of her murdered Uncle Jacob Turk. On the way up to the front door of the Golden Sickle the Major kept insisting on the murderous savagery of these men, a fact that Barbara and I knew well enough, as he went on explaining again how they had broken into his house and ransacked it and Elisha had cleverly come upon the box of clues and guessed its meaning and then they had waited in the house to surprise and murder the Major and Wherry who, unarmed and on their way back from Mister List's store at Grave Creek, had been forced to hide in the peach orchard till the pirates had, at last, given up and gone in pursuit of me and Barbara. But they had taken articles of clothing of both the Major and Wherry and, after breaking into the henhouse, had slaughtered two red roosters to

bloody them in preparation of Elisha's planned bluff against me. I remembered well the chicken feather that clung to the gore on the Major's bullet-riddled tricorne. I waited till he was done and then told him of Elisha's cunning unravelling of the two clues and his certainty that the "moon" beneath which the poem said the treasure lay hidden was most surely the crescent moon of the Golden Sickle itself.

"Ay, but where?" cried the Major, rubbing his frostbitten fingers. "I had already guessed where the treasure was, myself—I guessed it when I drew the false circle on that plagued map to lead them many leagues astray. Little did I reckon that that map would get you kidnapped, Dan'l boy. Kidnapped and maybe worse."

He cast a baleful glance at Barbara.

"Madam, I pardon you now—although what you did started out in the most villainous spirit. Even so—like many miscalculations—it had the happiest consequences: it saved young Dan'l's life and I thank you and Fortune herself for that."

He rubbed his forehead thoughtfully again.

"To be sure the treasure is hid beneath the Golden Sickle," said he. "But where? 'Tis a great sprawling quarters."

We stood now in the big common room, warming ourselves at the fine fire of fat pine logs which Wherry had kindled and then gone to stand watch in the north window of the hall that gave a clean view for a clear mile downriver.

"Any sight of the rascals?" called the Major.

"Not a flyspeck moves on yonder white ice," Wherry answered. "There be nothing stirring out yonder save an owl or two. And the west wind."

"Could they creep up on the house through the brush filth and under the shadow of trees?"

"Major," said Wherry earnestly, "me ears is gone to earth these long winters since Valley Forge. But me eyes is as good as ever they was when I stood night watch for the late General, God rest him in a patriot's paradise."

"Let me see the ring again, Dan'l," said the Major, scowling perplexedly. " 'Tis the third and last clue. It must hold the final answer."

When I had given it to him he polished it on his sleeve and held it up. Then he lit a candle from the fireplace and set the stick before him on the board, studying the ring in its spill of yellow light. We all gathered round him, except Sally who sat warming her hands on the bench by the fire, and we peered over his shoulder as he pondered it. It looked like the strangest ring the hand of man had ever fashioned. It was ancient, too; its moon face with glaring eyes and outstuck tongue shone with a luster of utmost antiquity. The Major's finger stroked the twin stars beneath the moonish mask and opposite these the space left in the silver, which formed a small short crescent. I will show it to you again—

"That crescent," murmured the Major. "It puts me plain in mind of something. I've seen a crescent like that somewheres about. But where? 'Tis not just any crescent, d'ye see? It's got a squarish tinge to it—and 'tis rough cornered. Still, it's a crescent for all that and it's silver, too."

From the hallway we heard a mutter from Wherry and all turned listening.

"Have they showed on the horizon?"

"No, Major. 'Twas nothing," answered the old soldier peevishly. " 'Twas only a fox after an owl at the corner of the south pasture. I wish it was them. I'd like to lay hands on that squidget of a dwarf. And for the rest of them I've got two good Philadelphy pistols and a horn of dry powder and enough balls in my coat pocket for the whole rapscallion pack of 'em!"

"Good," said the Major. "I think we could stand them off. But we still must hurry. God knows, if they do find themselves thwarted at the last—that dwarf might try to fire the place."

"He'll burn soon enough," said Barbara drily. "In a hotter place than he could ever kindle here for us."

"Ay, but we must hurry. Once we've laid hands on the treasure we can retreat back to my place. Wherry and Dan'l and I could stand them off better there, for we know the lay of things. This great sprawling place has too many crannies and secret ways and panelled places to suit my fancy."

And he set about puzzling over the ring again in the halo of candleshine.

My joy at being with Sally again was somehow full of the whole fresh joy of discovery. It was a feeling so keen that I could recall nothing like it before and I'm afraid I neglected my new friend Barbara just then, not to mention my failure to contribute anything helpful to the Major's riddling over of the ring.

I had joined Sally on the bench before the roaring fire, for we were both still chilled from the long ride, and soon I felt her shy fingers twine with my own. I said nothing of my loss of her locket, nor of Doctor Longo's ghastly wax image of her head, nor of any of the other creations in that strange, unforgettable gallery, though I did tell her some of my fears while I was there.

"I reckoned you were dead," I said.

She blushed in the firelight and it was one of those times when her dark eyes took on a bright liveliness that made it hard for me to believe that they were really eternally sightless.

"Would you have wept and carried on a whole lot if I had been dead, Dan'l?"

I felt a little choked at the thought.

"Sally, I can't tell you how terrible I felt," I said stumblingly.

"What was it like?" she said, zesting in it a little.

"It was like I'd gone blind, too," I said truthfully. "It was like all the light in the world snuffed out like a candle in the wind."

"My, that sure is beautiful," she said.

She sighed and her face looked marvelous happy, the way all girls get at the thought of being dead and missed and mourned over and still being alive to imagine it.

"Sally?"

"What, Dan?"

"Sally, I don't reckon a body appreciates somebody till they reckon they've lost them for good."

"That's so," she said. "When that lady took you away on her horse me and the Major figured you were a gonner."

"Did you cry?" I said eagerly.

"Cry? Why, I carried on so bad the Major had to fetch vinegar on a kerchief for my head."

I felt like the fire was getting too hot. I went around on the other side of the bench and sat down beside Sally again.

I must have cleared my throat six or eight times. It was the worst thing in the world trying to seize hold of words for what I wanted to say.

"Sally," I said directly. "It seems like you and me haven't understood each other too good here these past few months."

She thought about that a spell.

"Why, no," she said, smiling. "I've understood you always, Dan'l."

"You understood me when I was a child," I said. "But what you don't know is I've become a man here of late."

"I know it," she said, wonderfully.

"You couldn't have known it," I said. "It only just happened. It happened while I was tied up on that boat downriver."

"Well, it's been happening for a long time," she said with certainty. "I felt it begin to happen last summer."

"I tell you it just come over me all of a sudden," I said. "Tonight!"

"No," she said. "It happened last summer. I can even remember the day. I can remember the place, too."

"Where?"

"We were out in the garden," she said.

"You mean that time we swore we'd always be friends?" I said.

"Ay," she said.

"Oh, that was just a child's pledge," said I. "And I made it because I felt this strange new thing coming between us."

"You were growing up, Dan," she said. "So was I. That was the thing you felt. It was the day I first felt you were coming to manhood."

"Tut," said I. "You make too much of it, Sally."

"Didn't you mean it, Dan'l?"

"Ay, I did. Didn't I cut our fingers and tie them together till our bloods went a-mingling? Yet it was a child's pledge."

"Still and all, you swore," she said. "You said you swore by the moon, too."

"Ay. I mind that."

"And since it was broad day and no moon in the sky," she went on, "you swore by the great stone sickle moon."

"What sickle moon?"

"Why, the one that is set in the flagstones of the garden."

I held my breath.

"The sickle!" I whispered. "The moon!"

"What is it, Dan'l?" she cried, shaking my fingers. "Dan'l, what's wrong!"

"That moon!" I cried. "That stone sickle in the garden, Sally! Why, 'tis the one Pap meant, I think! Major! Major! I reckon I know where the third clue points!"

And at my great hubbub Wherry came a-running and Barbara sprang near and the Major sent Wherry to fetch spades and a mattock and we were soon all crowding out through the pantry door into the cold again, into the moonlit garden. All of it lay round about, snowbound and shadowed in blue and lavender. The cold winter rose bushes—including poor Meg's great General Washington bush—stood about pruned and barren. The old apple tree held the new moon caught in its twisty branches and stars shone through the twined trellises of the scuppernong vines.

Much as I was excited about finding the treasure, there was a matter more urgent in my thoughts. I went to Barbara, who was standing back, arms folded, watching the progress of the Major and Wherry as they scraped at the snow with their spades.

"Barbary?"

"Ay, Dan lad."

"Don't tell," I whispered.

"Don't tell what, Dan boy," she said.

"About that kiss," I said. "It would hurt Sally something fierce."

"I won't," she promised and squeezed my hand.

The Major stopped shoveling back snow and held up his hand.

"Hold," said he. "We must take our soundings soundly. We're going about this too hastily."

And he held the lantern high in one hand and the silver ring in the other and studied it in the mingled light of whale oil and moon.

"Now, fetch me the spool of leadsman's twine, Dan'l," he said, and I did that and he went and had Wherry fetch a broom from the kitchen and he went to sweeping snow aside in a great fury. At last we all stared down at it—the great pale sandstone sickle moon set among the irregular flat flags.

"Then the treasure is hid under there?" I whispered in the tense stillness.

"Why, no, lad," said the Major shrewdly. "Don't ye see? This sickle is a small part of a greater circle, like every sickle is—even the moon in her quarters. By the curve of the moon's thin phase we could judge the size of that great night Queen herself—even if we'd never seen her at the full. D'ye follow?"

"I reckon so. But then how do we calculate where to dig, sir?"

"Tut, boy. Let me proceed. We must find the precise curve of this arc and then determine its center and when we've found its center we can discover its fullness. That's what the twine is for. Stand yonder, Dan'l, and hold the spool while I unwind it. Ay, stand square in the midst of the stone sickle, boy. That's right. Now we find the center."

And when he had found that center, which was as far as the twine would stretch, he bade me go stand there and hold the other end of the thick cord while he swung it round in a great huge orbit that fitted the curve of the stone sickle moon herself—a swing that encompassed the whole of the garden within its moon-shadowed walls.

"Resuming now," said he. "We have this great huge circumference which the sickle moon yonder has determined. Let us now fancy it as the great face of a clock."

"A clock?" said Barbara.

"Why?" said I.

"Because," quoth he. " 'There is no scoundrel still alive —Knows these lie where the Hand is at Five.' "

It was simple from that point. Taking the center of the sandstone sickle as midnight, it turned out that the spot where Five would lie was a shallow place under the very shadow of the small damson tree where Sally and I had used to sit, on summer days, playing cat's cradle. The Major stamped his foot on the stones and rang the mattock loud.

"We dig here!" he cried.

There were only two spades and the four of us took turns digging, which was stiff going near the surface where the earth was frozen hard as stale biscuit bread, and after a long spell a great hole yawned and not a sign of anything but a few poor homeless summer worms and a handful of delicate Indian birdpoint flints.

"Something's amiss. We've read it wrong," said the Major presently, wiping his brow which was, like ours, sweating despite the crackling cold night air.

"Ay," said Sally soundly from the shadows. "That's because you've not heeded the verse properly."

"What are you getting at, gal?"

" 'Mark not the Phase which Only seems—But under the sway of Pollux beams,' " she quoted from rote, and it seemed to us then that a blind child might have had better eyes than any of ours.

"The child is right," cried the Major, stabbing his spade upright in the great heap of dark earth we had made.

"How so, sir?" said I.

The Major chuckled.

"Don't you mind, lad, what I said to you that night about a Truth being hidden beneath a Truth and that first Truth being false?"

"Ay."

"I should not have stopped there," said he. "I should have reminded both of us that a third Truth sometimes lies buried deeper yet."

"How so, sir?"

"Why, looky here, Dan'l," he said, and held up the glittering thing in one hand and swung down the lantern with the other until the grimacing face shone plain. "The ring," said he. "Ay, the ring holds the answer. The ring was the only true clue all along."

"Then what did all the rest of it mean?" I cried, a little impatiently. "What of the spool and the bidding of the poem?"

"I may be mistaken," said the Major. "But I'll wager

that the poem is like most riddles—it depends on which way you look at it. And I'd bet my life that the spool was meant to do what I meant that map to do—to send fools on a fools' chase. There's more layers to this than rings in a tree!"

"You mean Pap meant someone to measure with the cord like we did?"

"Ay, he did."

"To measure and find—"

"Nothing," said the Major. "And there's no clue left—unless we look closely. Unless we look at the ring very, very closely."

He beckoned us all round again as he held the ring up in the circle of lanternshine.

"Look ye at the ring," said he. "There's a crescent here —d'ye see? Beside the Gorgon's face. Ay, and two little stars beneath it, like stars beneath the moon."

"That's the twins," said Sally. "Castor and Pollux. I've never seen them. But I dreamed of them once."

"I well believe that," cried the Major. "And your woman's good sense may have set us aright."

He pointed to the ring again, tapping it excitely with his finger.

"Now mind how the verse goes on," said he. " 'Heed not wrong'—that means the false turn we took—'But Hew to the Right'—and that, unless I miss my guess, means the right-hand star—here beside the crescent. See? 'Tis stamped in the soft silver."

We all agreed, gathering around more closely and hoping that he was right this time.

"Now if we hold this crescent on the ring to correspond to the crescent yonder in the stones," said he. "Then the treasure must lie beneath the point where that small right-hand star signifies. Like the poem said—'Under the sway of Pollux beams.' Let's see if that's so. It's a desperate guess but I think we may be close upon it, at last. Lend a speedy hand here. Quick. Those scoundrels may be yonder on the riverbank by now. Come—Quick! Swing the mattock, Wherry! Up with those flagstones. Dig, lads, dig!"

We dug for what seemed a small eternity.

"Ho! What's this? What's this!"

There is no noise on this earth quite the same as that drummish, hollow utterance that a spade brings forth from a buried box; there is no sound, for treasure seekers, quite so pulse-quickening. Nor is there any color quite the same as the reddish-yellow glint of gold struck aslant by the mingling of moon and lanternshine.

In a moment the small, brass-bound chest lay open before us and we stood staring down at its cold, shining contents: six bars of yellow gold to the weight of thirty, three bars of silver of forty weight, and eight small bags of French and Spanish coin.

We stood about oohing and ahhing, so spellbound by the gold that, for a while, none of us remembered the priceless string of pearls. It was at last Barbara who, rather wistfully, asked if they were there.

"Nary a sign of them," sighed the Major, feeling the small leather bags to see if they might have been secreted among the coins. "Still and all there's a fortune in gold here alone. I reckon we shouldn't be too greedy. Still, it is strange that the pearls should not be here."

"Wait!" I said, suddenly remembering the dwarf's shrewd words back on Doctor Longo's boat. "Look more closely, sir. Is there no sign of a wine bottle in the chest?"

"What, boy?"

"Wine, sir. A bottle of Madeira perhaps?—Among the bags of coin?"

"Wine. What's this talk of wine, lad?"

And I told him the dwarf's cunning translation of the lines of the poem which had run: "Queen of Batavia, helter skelter—Fled to Madeira's glassy shelter."

At this fresh clue the Major raised the chest out onto the snow-covered flagstones and dug a little farther into the dark, fresh earth beneath which it had rested.

" 'Tis a fresh riddle," said he, at last. "I've dug another foot and heard not so much as a clink."

Again it was Sally's quick wit which saved us.

"If I were to be searching for a bottle of wine," said she, "I'd sure be looking in a different sort of hole from that."

"What do you mean, Sally?"

"Why, I'd search for wine in a wine cellar," she said, with a laugh.

That made the best sense in the world and the Major harumphed and looked red and we grabbed up the chest between us and made off in that direction. There was an old, heavy trapdoor to the wine cellar, set into the foundations beneath the Golden Sickle's pantry. The door, set into an angle of thick masonry just under the pantry wall, was stuck tight with snow which had melted and frozen again, but Wherry chipped and pried it open with his mattock and we entered, the Major leading the way and holding the lantern high.

The wine cellar had been seldom used in the years since my father had built the great tavern. In these late days most rough travellers on the river road had no such fine palates as crave fancy, old wines, preferring to take with their meals usquebaugh or whisky and sometimes applejack or the cheap peach brandy which Jacob Turk used to make and store to be tapped out of great hogsheads in a chamber off the pantry. The wine cellar of the Golden Sickle looked as if it had not been entered since creation began. I reflected sadly of those old times when, perhaps, gentlemen and ladies had come to the Golden Sickle to visit my charming father and I could imagine his being the last to enter this wine cellar before tonight, perhaps to fetch up a rare old bottle of Fundador to serve his gentry friends. The shelves were as numerous as the tubes of a honeycomb and each was set aslant into the walls so that the bottles were basketed at the proper angle. The Major drew out several, sleeved away the dust, and studied the labels. Wherry read over his shoulder and gave a grumbling laugh.

"Not much to go by," said he. "They all seem to be Madeira."

" 'Tis a fine riddle, indeed," laughed the Major. "Shall we drink every bottle empty, all to find a mere string of beads? And who'll be sober enough when that's done to know beads from cobwebs!"

He fetched out another bottle and studied it more closely.

"Tut," said he. "What's wanted now is a smidgen of wit."

A thousand or more bottles of Madeira, I thought with bewilderment. And one containing a priceless rope of pearls. But which?

At that moment all our thoughts were interrupted. Unmistakably, the faintest draft of air stirred in the breathless cellar; the flame in the lantern staggered and dipped and lay aslant a moment or so before it righted again and burned on steady. At this we all grew still and the Major glanced toward the bevelled stone archway of the outer exit beyond which darkness lay like a river of ink.

"Where does that lead, Dan lad?"

" 'Tis a tunnel, sir," I whispered. "It leads to that thick-doored opening beneath the big willow on the riverbank just below the road."

"Who used it?"

"Why, in the old days the smugglers used it, sir," I said.

"For what? Do ye know what, boy?"

"Why, I've heard tell they'd scuttle keelboats yonder at the Devil's Elbow," said I. "Then bring their booty here. All kinds of Pittsburgh goods. And sometimes stolen slaves."

"Then these rogues might know of this?"

"Elisha and his gang know very few of the secret passage-ways in the Golden Sickle, sir, and they are many. I reckon Pap built it that way—not trusting them much."

"But they might know of this main one," said the Major, gripping his pistol and eyeing the black tunnel in readiness.

"Ay, they might remember it, sir."

I took the ring of the lantern from his grasp and went to the archway with it. I held it high and peered down the gutlike tunnel. The passage was a straight one, making no turns, though dimpled along its sides with a score or more of small sidelong nooks. The lantern's dim rays cast a light a long ways into its hollow deeps and I saw no one there as far as I could see, not even the telltale lace of a sleeve of someone hid in one of the side wall crannies. I told the Major I thought no one was there.

"Tut, boy," he said, grabbing my sleeve. "That's folly to stand like that. You're a pointblank target framed there in the archway."

I shrugged and stepped away and set the lantern on the treasure chest.

"Still, sir," said I. "I think it was only the wind that made the lamp flame gutter so. This whole great house has more small random winds and drafts than the Seven Seas in an old map."

"Perhaps," said the Major, suspiciously. "But you, Wherry—Keep a weather eye on that entrance while we set about trying to unravel this riddle of the wine."

"Ay, sir," said the old soldier, his eye aglint with what I suspected was a hunger for some pistol play and mischief as he set himself on an old Dupont powderbox, with the long pistol eased up on one knee and his jaw abulge with a twist of Maryland kitefoot.

Major Henthorn sat himself beside the lantern on the treasure chest. He stared at the bottle of wine in his hand and sighed. Then he chuckled and thrust his thumbs up on the cork till it popped and it was a pleasant sound in that gravelike stillness of the cellar.

"I'll wager a round of wine may sharpen our judgment on this matter," said he, passing the bottle to Barbara. "Since it's wine the riddle hinges on."

We all had a sip and felt the better for it though it did not seem to conjure up any miracles of insight. Not immediately, that is.

"A grand year," said the Major, wiping his lips with his cambric kerchief and studying the label again. "Vinho Madeira 1772—"

"Cidade Funchal," said I over his shoulder, spelling the faded words out carefully and slowly, having had enough trouble with the reading of American without giving time to these outlandish Roman words.

"Cidade Funchal," I said again, proudly. "Is that the brand of the wine, sir?"

"Why, no, boy," said the Major with an impatient scowl like a piqued schoolmaster. " 'Tis the capital city of those islands—Cidade Funchal."

He studied the label some more and pointed a finger.

"Here, lad," said he. "Here's the brand of the vintner—Meio-dia."

"Noonday," said Wherry absently, and whistled a bar of an old militia quickstep all out of tune but spirited, his warlike eye still fixed eager on the passageway.

"What say, Wherry?" said the Major, with a sidelong glance at him, half thinking he might be signalling an appearance of the river pirates in the tunnel.

"Noonday," Wherry said again. "Meio-dia. I'd not likely soon forget that, Major."

" 'Tis an odd, alien word, Wherry. How do you come to remember it?"

"Because I sailed on a Portuguee frigate once," said Wherry. "We sailed out of Cape Hatteras when I was still a fresh chap not long out of Norfolk orphanage. Many's and many's the watch I stood on our fair passage down to Bahia. That's in Brazil, sir, and 'tis Portuguee land, too, sir, and a main wild, vast land it is, sir—half heathen injun and half Popish. And I'd stand my turn of watch many's and many's the morn till meio-dia—that's noonday, as I say, sir. Meia-noite. That's midnight. Well I remember. 'Twas on return from that voyage that I seen the broadside in Boston town calling for volunteers to fight the British. And then—"

He broke off his reminiscing then and shook his head and stroked his tough-set, grizzled cheek, smiling at his thoughts of those rough-and-tumble times.

"Meio-dia," Wherry said in a fond, soft singsong. "Meio-dia. And fair noondays they was in those warm, wild oceans. Not like the weather of these landlocked mountains."

If the rest of us shared for the moment Wherry's dream of warm tropical isles, the Major was not listening. His face was thunderstruck with thought and he had picked up the spent cork of our Christmas night bottle and sat staring at it as if he held a diamond in his fingers.

"What's wrong, sir?" said I, with a fading smile.

"Wrong?" he laughed softly. "Why right is the word—not wrong. I think our bold, fine friend Wherry here can claim to have found our necklace for us. Looky here!"

We gathered close around in the circle of light and—those of us with eyes to see—stared at the time-darkened cork in the Major's hand. With his other finger he was pointing to the device which, burned into the top of it, like the brand on the hide of a bull, showed the face of a clock with both hands pointing to twelve. It was faint but it was unmistakable.

I was the first to run to the shelves of bottles and stared round at them in bewilderment. A thousand bottles, a thousand corks, and each one burned with the same clock's brand of Noonday.

"They're all the same, sir," I exclaimed, scowling perplexedly.

"Tut, now! I'll wager not!" cried the Major, who was at my side now, the lantern held high as he ran his fingers up and down the bottles from cork to cork. "I'll wager my share of yonder gold that there is one cork here with a clock burned in that's different. Come help me search. All eyes, hurry."

"How shall we know it?" asked Barbara, her eyes warming at the thought of the pearls.

"Why, that's plain enough, madam," cried the Major with a proud glance at old Wherry who, planted on his box a little to one side of the tunnel's mouth, kept his sharp eye fixed fiercely on the darkness and paid no heed to our games.

"Look ye for the cork with the different clock on it," cried the Major.

"How different?"

"Why, 'twill be the clock that shows where the hand is at five," cried he. "That's what the verse was trying to tell us up yonder in the garden. Those last lines pertain to the last and richest part of the treasure. 'There is no scoundrel still alive—Knows these'—meaning the pearls—'Knows these lie where the Hand is at Five.' Quick now. Search, all. The eye that spies the Hand at Five—he will have found the Queen of Batavia!"

At that moment, faintly, the sound of a pebble dislodged and fell, ringing deep within the black passage, a damp, dim sound like a stone dropped in a well.

"I've found it! I've found it!" I cried at that very instant and, lifting the bottle reverently out, I stared at the cork again which, sure enough, different from its thousand dusty mates, was branded plainly with the small clock showing five. Before I could raise the bottle against the lantern light to peer through its winy twilight to see, at last, the hidden pearls I heard the sharp intake of breath behind me.

"Is it them?" whispered the Major, turning.

Wherry crouched lower against the jamb of the stone archway with his cocked pistol held at the ready and the victory of the moment was somewhat undone by that obscure alarm.

"Is it them?"

"It mought well be," Wherry said in a soft, savage voice.

"And it mought have been rats. But the way I sees it 'twill be rats in ary case."

"Stand behind those shelves," said the Major, leading Sally to that shelter.

He motioned to Barbara. "And you, madam," he said, bowing. "Take refuge with the child."

Barbara glared at him a moment.

"D'ye trust me with a pistol, sir?" she said. "I see you have an extry in your belt."

"Why, madam?"

"I'd like a chance to prove myself a friend," she said.

The Major smiled and handed her the other pistol without blinking an eye, for he was not a man to waste time in judgments of trustworthiness and character.

"You've already proven that," he said. "But we can use your help if those rascals are preparing to come storming out of yonder tunnel."

"If they're yonder," said Wherry in a voice that quivered with hopefulness, "they'll show at any minute. And I'd counsel them to come a-firing, for it's fire and balls they'll meet."

At that moment came a heavy crash above us and a choir of cursing, heavy voices.

"Why, no," said the Major. "That's them in the rooms above."

And small dribs of dust came sifting down on us as heavy boots rang striding and stomping about on the floor of the common room, which I judged to be just over our heads, for the base of its great chimney formed part of the wine cellar's wall and we could hear now the hoarse, angry voices of Prettijohn and Blue cursing and kicking open doors and overturning tables and chairs.

"It's us they're seeking," I whispered, with a shiver.

"Why, no," said the Major, holding his hand to his cocked ear. "Use your ears, lad. 'Tis not our names they're cursing after, at all."

"Then who?"

"Why, from the sound of it, 'tis the dwarf," said he.

"Ay, 'tis Elisha they're after," said Barbara, smiling grimly. "He's betrayed his chums as usual."

And sure enough as we listened we could hear them as they hailed and hollered and shouted the name of Elisha—coupled with other words I'll not repeat—from one end of the Golden Sickle to the other.

" 'Tis like him," said Barbara, still smiling fiercely. "He's tricking them again."

"Then if he's not with them—" said I to all who had turned from the tunnel's mouth and lifted their faces to the drumming hubbub above, "—If he's not up there with them—where is he?"

Wherry, too, in that fatal moment had turned his eyes from the passageway and stared up at the dust-raining ceiling with the rest of us.

The sound as it flew from the tunnel's mouth was almost silent: like the soft, silver whir of a white pigeon's wings—the sword from the dwarf's walking stick that came, swift as an arrow, from the darkness and—with the thud like the single blow that drives a nail—pinned Wherry's arm to the wooden wall that stretched beyond the shelves.

Wherry's face blanched and bowed grimacing in the agony of that moment and as the sword, which had transfixed his arm, whirred in its target like the thrum of Prettijohn's Jew's harp the big pistol fell with a clatter from his nerveless fingers. By a miracle it had not discharged but lay there on the dusty boards and as I ran to fetch it up from beneath the archway a long arm sprang from the shadows and dragged me up so close that I could feel both the cold ring of the pistol in the flesh behind my ear and the heat of the dwarf's breath on my cheek as he whispered.

"Move so much as a thumb to cock those pistols and this boy is dead," he said softly.

"I reckon he means it, Major," I said in a voice that sounded like a sob, not so much from fear as from the choking of my collar gripped so tight.

"Ay, Dan. Let him take what he wants."

"That's marvelous good sense," sneered the dwarf. "And surprising to hear from a Yorkshireman!"

Still, it was touch and go, it was tit for tat; for it was plain sense that if the pirates heard a pistol shot from the wine cellar Elisha's jigs would have been up no less than ours. And he wanted none of that since he was plainly up to some extempore mischief of his own and meant his chums upstairs to share no part of his under-staircase venture.

"Mind now, Englishman. And you, lady gay. No monkeyshines or the boy is deader than Adam!"

The Major and the dwarf's erstwhile lady both nodded and tossed their uncocked pistols on the cellar floor. Poor Wherry leaned into the wall as if half crucified: sweat stood on his forehead and his pierced and transfixed arm dribbled red that ran in a ribbon down the wooden bulwark wall. He glared coldly at the dwarf while, soundlessly, his mouth shaped the hearty curses of his old and half-forgotten soldiery. But he, like the others, made not so much as a glance at the three pistols on the floor.

Elisha glanced swiftly at the box on the floor. The chest was plainly what he sought, for it was obviously fresh unearthed, still bearing, on its brass-bound top, traces of garden soil. Still dragging me before him like a toy in his powerful grasp Elisha kicked the lid open with his boot toe and knelt, holding me up as a shield, and commenced stuffing the chest's contents—bar and bag—into the capacious pockets of his greatcoat. The coat was of strong stuff—stout as moneybag cloth—and it began to sag as he continued.

"I'll kill this Cresap cub if you so much as wink an eye at those pistols," he said as he went busily on about the filling of his pockets, though not without a touchy glance upward at the sounds of the savage and redoubled hue and cry which the others were lifting against him.

"Fire the house!" cried a bawling voice from somewhere afar in the rooms.

"Ay, fire the bloody place with him in it!"

"Ay, we'll have that satisfaction!" yelled another. "And we can sift the ashes after for the gold."

"But what of them pearls?"

"Ay, what of the pearls? Won't pearls burn up?"

"Devil take the pearls! Pearls is woman's truck, I say!"

"Ay, that's so, Sawney!" cried the voice I knew to be Blue's. "The feel of gold—that's proper metal for the hands of a man. Fire the house, I say. Here, Prettijohn, fetch me tow and a torch! Here's whale oil aplenty!"

In the corner of my eye I caught Elisha's face and saw it blanch at the name of that thing called Fire and I even heard the soft intake of his breath, though the steely arm which gripped my neck like the scruff of a pup did not quaver a hair nor, in the same hand, did the muzzle of the cocked pistol at my head. He had plucked the treasure chest clean as a bone by now, it was all in his clothes, and in the box there remained not so much as gold-dust grain nor stiver of coin. He advanced now a pace upon the others, thrusting me so hard before him that I caught my breath and rolled my eyes and felt the ring of the pistol press harder into the skin behind my ear. Though now Elisha's voice was soft and nastily courteous.

"Now I reckon I'll have a little wine," he said. "For I overheard your talk as I lay creeping in yonder tunnel. Wine, please."

He shook with soundless laughter.

"A little wine," he said. "A fine bottle of Funchal Madeira. Five o'clock brand, I'd say. Ay, 'tis a good year that. Fetch it across to me. That's so that when I'm gone I may drink a toast to the poor fools who've made a rich man of me. That's proper, eh? Don't that seem only fit comportment for a gentleman like me? To drink a toast to his benefactors? Eh?"

"Fire the place!" Prettijohn's voice kept bawling from the common room above. "Ay, that's proper. Spill a bit more oil over yonder. Splash it round good."

Elisha's grip did not weaken by a screw but I could feel his whole body shudder strongly as there came plain to all our ears the first faint drumming voice of a gathering conflagration. In the corner of my eye I saw his face shoot upward for a quick glance at the dusty cracks in the ceiling from which now—in myriad tiny wreaths—gray smoke crawled and walked like spiders upon the boards.

"Hurry!" he cried, shaking me like a rat. "The pearls! The bottle with the pearls!"

Without an instant's hesitation, Major Henthorn stepped forward, proferring the fateful bottle of Madeira.

"No tricks, Englishman," said Elisha. "I'll soon see if they're there or not."

"They are there," said the Major with a strange smile.

"No tricks, I say. Let me see."

"You may see," said the Major. "I have looked and I have seen. You have my word as officer and gentleman that the necklace called the Queen of Batavia is in this bottle of wine."

Elisha held his free hand out to take it.

"Splash more oil! Here. These big cracks yonder. Here!" cried Blue's voice from immediately above us. And at the very moment when Elisha reached for the bottle it happened. In dreams long since that strange Christmas night I have seen the way in which that fiery, blazing liquid—as if poured down in some rendered judgment from Heaven—streamed down in twin columns of flaming rain upon the dwarf and myself. In other dreams to come I shall always hear his awful, bestial scream of terror and pain, for the blazing whale oil which Prettijohn or Sawney had poured through the wide cracks of the old common-room floor splashed mostly upon the dwarf and, when he thrust me stumbling from him across the damp floor of the wine cellar the flames in my own clothes were mainly extinguished. He had turned away now, reeling and smoking and cursing. In the archway—as if in some savage afterthought—he turned and fired the pistol blindly: a shot which missed us all, it seemed, but which sent a dozen bottles of wine exploding upon each other in a splinter cascade down the shelves behind which Sally had taken shelter. Still badly burned and smoking, he had another pistol out of his belt in a twinkling and aimed it at the Major's breast.

"Fetch me that bottle!" he screamed. "The pearls! I'll have those pearls if I burn in Hell for them!"

At that, as if in answer from some awful higher judgment, a fresh stream of burning oil fell splattering across the whole front of him and he turned stumbling into the tunnel and was gone amid the racketing echo of his screams.

At that point Wherry cursed and with his free hand

reached up stoutly and set his grip soundly round the blade which transfixed his arm. For a moment the veins stood on his forehead as he strained hard before it sprang free from the wood and he plucked it out of his flesh. Then he fell a-cursing upon his pistol and was halfway to the archway when the Major's cry stopped him.

"Stay, Wherry!" he shouted. "Look at him yonder. He's a dead man already. Don't waste your shot."

We clustered together round the tunnel's mouth watching him go. The rough stone walls were lit as that squat scarlet figure passed flaming down them. He staggered from wall to wall, borne down and made awkward by the extra weight of the gold amid his clothes, and his voice kept up its demon's chant of screams all the way to the small and distant end. His endurance was, for all that, astonishing, for he went the whole tunnel's quarter-mile length in flames and burst out, at last, from the tiny door at its diminished end and still went on, as if kept alive by sheer demon fury, and strutted out onto the river ice which was already bright with the first pale flush of sunrise. And then—miraculously —amid that first fresh light he vanished. He was there one moment, wallowing in flames beneath his weight of gold, and in the next second—as if by magic—he was gone, leaving in the air above him only a curl or two of smoke to wreathe and dissipate itself among those last few shreds of that night's river fog.

Behind us the Golden Sickle blazed furiously against that gray sky of eastern morning as we followed Wherry to a place on the thick river ice where he now stood staring down. Black river water coursed swiftly beneath the clean break in the ice where Elisha had gone through.

"Cat ice," he said again. "And quarter less twain of river to the bottom."

Barbara shuddered and squeezed Wherry's hand.

"And in the same hole he cut last night for another man," she said.

Wherry cast a glance toward the building, which burned brightly far up behind the cluster of sheltering willows. He twisted more tightly the kerchief Barbara had given him to tie about the arm above his wound. We could all see the pirates gathered round the pyre of the Golden Sickle, though they could not see us.

"Well, we've lost a treasure," said Wherry, in a gesture as if dusting his hands: the act of a poor man who has seen many coins come and go between his honest fingers and who thinks little amiss of one more coin or many gone with the others.

"Ay," we heard the Major's voice call softly from the riverbank behind us. "Ay, I think we've lost a treasure indeed."

He had stayed behind us when we left the wine cellar and had been a long time following. Now he stood beneath the old willow which towered above the tunnel's stony entrance.

"I think we have lost more of a treasure than we know," he said and we all moved closer to see the poor sad sight which lay in his arms.

With a cry of despair I ran to her.

It was Sally, limp as Death itself, her whole face and breast all ribboning with blood and a great ridge in her scalp from the dwarf's last pistol ball.

THE bottle of Madeira with its precious content of pearls stood on the thick-legged, carved Tudor table by the window of Major Henthorn's own bedroom. It shone, dark as a vessel of blood, in the pale cold dawn of that morning of Saint Stephen's Day. Yet none of us gave it so much as a glance, nor thought, nor twitch of speculation. We sat grouped round, hushed and solemn-faced, at the great English bed in whose deep goosedown tick and beneath the faded quilts and comforters of Major Henthorn's own long-dead mother, lay Sally Cecil.

Old Doctor Grindstaff, who had been fetched on horse-back all the way downriver from Elizabethtown by Wherry himself, stood by the bed looking down purse-lipped at the small, round face framed in its thick swaddling of clean white bandages torn from clean sheets. He was a good old man with the face of a judicious walrus and the grave black clothes of a Quaker. He tilted the flat Friends' hat in his hands, tapping the brim thoughtfully with his pale, nervous fingers.

"I cannot tell thee more than that," he concluded. "This afternoon should prove the turning. 'Tis the way with children. Thee hath seen it happen and so have I, many's the time. They rally suddenly—or they die as quick."

He measured and poured some tinctures in a goblet and left the room.

" 'Twill be best if thee leave her alone," he said to us before he went off again with Wherry into the fresh new snowfall that had commenced against the gray winter landscape.

Yonder on the slope of land above the river road lay the black smoking ruins that had once been the Golden Sickle. Behind it on the garden wall, kicking their boots idly in a row, sat three figures that I took to be Sawney, Blue, and Prettijohn—waiting till the ashes should cool so that they might sift them for the vanished gold. Long might they search, thought I, nor find much more than a bit of melted pewter here and there or maybe one of Meg's old silver spoons. I watched Wherry and the doctor ride back to Elizabethtown through the streaks of fresh falling snow.

Barbara and the Major stood at the foot of the great bed, staring at Sally and, I reckon, each praying in his way. I was overcome with the sudden impulse of wanting to be alone with her: she was all I had had, we had grown up together and shared all of life's small pleasures and misfortunes mostly alone; it seemed to me that we should be left alone together to share this one. These were a curious tug of feelings, for I loved Major Henthorn, too, and I had grown passing fond of Barbara. Yet I told them my sentiments—awkwardly, I suppose—and they graciously went out of the room.

Sally's small face seemed whiter than the snow which gathered afresh upon the sill beyond the quartered win-

dows. And as I drew to her side and clasped her hand there came to my mind the old song she had used to sing, the old singing game her voice had used to play as she wandered alone down the lonely chambers and passageways of the Golden Sickle.

"Lady Hamilton?" I whispered.

But not so much as an eyelid fluttered at my query.

I squeezed her hand closer to me and put my mouth nearer to her ear and shut my eyes and commenced the old song she had loved to sing in the dusks and twilights of that lost house.

> You must not put on your robes of black
> Nor yet your   bes of brown, O
> But you must put on your yellow gold stuffs
> To shine through Edinburgh town, O.

I fancied that the faintest flush of color shone on her cheek. Though it might have been a shadow cast by the corner of the great thick English quilt beneath her chin. I drew it down so her face would be clear of it and sang again in my child's croaking singsong, for I was never the sweet ballet singer that was she.

> Down came the old Queen
> Gold tassels in her hair
> O, Lady Hamilton, where's your babe
> I heared it greet so sair?

Yet not so much as a quiver on that still, pale mask.

I went slowly from the bedside and stood a moment staring at the bottle of Madeira which glowed like a ruby in the pale winter light. I fairly cursed it for all the treasure of the Queen of Batavia within it. If we had not gone into the wine cellar, if we had not found that bitter bottle, Sally would likely be up with us on this day after Christmas, laughing with us philosophically over our loss of the gold and smiling at the queer fortunes of give-and-take in this world's venturings to and fro.

I shut my eyes and prayed a hard, awkward prayer for Sally's life and I would gladly have taken the bottle of Madeira and all of its pearls and pitched it crashing through one of the panes of the window if it would have seemed just then, to Providence, an equitable trade. I glanced round at Sally again when I was done. Her face seemed unchanged.

"Lady Hamilton?" I said again in a creaking, querulous voice and tried to remember another bit of her song.

> Last night there were four Maries
> Tonight there'll be but three
> There was Mary Seaton and Mary Beaton
> And Mary Carmichael and me.

I shivered when I was done, for that verse seemed the one most filled with doom and I sat again in despair on the three-legged stool before the hearth, staring hopelessly into the warm, crackling log fire.

It seemed I sat there for hours and from time to time I could hear the hushed, grave voices of my friends in the house below me. I thought of all the wild, strange adventures those past three days had cast us among, and in my fancy in the shapes and colors of the flames I seemed to see again the face of the poor Frenchman Tailleferre on the night when he had come to me in the attic of the Golden Sickle, and I saw once more the image of the terrible dwarf and all his chums and the falling, strange figures of wax on the houseboat of Doctor Longo, and I even saw the brief red glint of the buried gold which had come so quickly among us and left us swift when the dwarf took it with him into the cold, dispersing waters of the river.

I had stared into the fire till my eyes watered and, I reckon, from time to time, I prayed though I was no great hand at such matters, having nothing much of religion in my recollection, as I have said before, but the long grace which Major Henthorn used to say at Sunday supper. It seemed I had wakened from a dream when I heard her voice speak clear in the room.

"Dan'l Cresap, I always did know the color of your hair."

I did not move at first, I did not take my gaze away from the crackling sticks on the iron dogs. I sat very still with my knees pressed together and my hands clenched upon them, thinking for sure that Sally had at last died and it was her ghost which I had heard. We were all quite accustomed to ghosts that spoke in those parts and in those times, so you need not think the fancy such a wild one.

Then I turned and saw Sally. She had sat up straight in the bed and was blinking and shielding her eyes in a strange way that I had never seen her do. Now she stared at me through the lattice of her fingers and laughed aloud.

"It's all so bright!" she exclaimed. "Will I ever get used to it?"

And with that she jumped out of the Major's great bed like I have heard some children do on Christmas morning and went running around the cold, bare floor in her nightdress and plucking up strange things to stare at: paperweight and prayerbook and pewter candlestick and blinking at them as if each was a fresh, remarkable toy. I sat gawping in stunned wonder, not sure yet whether I was seeing shade or substance. And when she turned to me and stared square at me and held out her arms with tears shining in her bright and plainly seeing eyes I let out a yell and fled to the head of the stairs.

"Major Henthorn! Major Henthorn!"

He and Barbara and Wherry came up the staircase at a bound and into the room. It was a great effort to get Sally back into the bed though the very exertion had somehow brought color back to her face and she was clearly out of danger. The magic of her restored sight which the grazing blow of Elisha's bullet had brought about left all of us humble and silent for a great while.

"We've gained this treasure," said the Major at last. "Whatever else we've had and lost."

"And we have the pearls," said I, noticing Barbara's steady stare at the bottle which shone on the bright table by the window.

"Ay, we have the pearls," said the Major, with a strange smile, and fetching the bottle up uncorked it with his thumbs.

"And will we share them?" said Barbara with a queer, skeptical smile.

"To be sure we'll share them, madam," said he, fetching five small wine glasses from the blue-painted wooden cupboard between the windows.

"Are the pearls really there?" said Sally from the bed. "Are they really in the wine?"

"Ay, child," said the Major. "They are in the wine."

And he poured the five small glasses full and handed one to Barbara and Sally and Wherry and me.

"Drink," smiled Major Henthorn. "Even if it is a little tart to the tongue. Drink the Madeira, my friends. For you may travel many's the mile and many's the year before you savor a costlier vintage."

While we drank Barbara could hold back no longer. She ran to the half-empty bottle and shook it against the light.

"Why, there's only a knotted cord in here," she said. "The pearls are gone!"

"The pearls are there, madam," said the Major. "We've already drunk half of them."

"What do you mean?" she cried.

"The ancients told of it in their chronicles," said the Major. "How Roman emperors used to dissolve pearls in sour wine and drink them as a toast to wastefulness. The Queen of Batavia had dissolved in this half-turned wine within a year after this lad's poor father put it there."

He fetched a candle snuffer from the mantelpiece then and fished out the knotted silken cord upon which the queen's ransom in pearls had once been strung.

Wherry grunted and went for the doorway, grumbling words to the effect that pearls were not meant for men anyway and that, whatever their worth in shillings, they were still a woman's fanglement and not worth troubling about.

Barbara stared a moment at the wet, empty circlet of string and then began to shout with hearty laughter; she laughed till her eyes streamed tears and then presently she sobered and stared at the Major almost tenderly. She held out her hand.

"May I have at least the string?" she said.

"Madam, for what purpose?" smiled the Major.

"As a remembrance."

"If you wish."

As he gave it to her he shot her a glance that was sharp though not unkindly.

"Didn't you mean to have it from the first?" he asked softly.

Barbara shrugged and she bowed her face, coloring a little.

"I would lie if I said I didn't," she murmured. "And I would as much hate lying to true friends as robbing them."

Later that afternoon when a snowy dusk was once more

settling across the bottomlands Barbara stood by the great front door, dressed for the road again. She smiled at Sally and me as she twisted the empty string wistfully round and round her fingers.

"I'm glad the string was empty."

"Why, Barbary?"

"Never mind why. Just bid me farewell and good riding. There's a fresh storm blowing from the west."

"Why do you go, Barbary?"

"Why should I stay?"

"We're true friends," said I.

"The road calls me," she said sharply. "And this great place purely frightens me."

"In what way?"

She smiled and turned her gaze to the blowing snow beyond the quartered window.

"Why, if I stayed," she said, "I might be sore tempted."

"To what, madam?" asked the Major.

She shot him a quick glance and then looked back to the window with a smile.

"Why," she laughed. "I might rob you of your bachelor's freedom, sir. And I am robber of quite another sort."

She pondered.

"Besides," she went on thoughtfully, still smiling, "I reckon you will do better by yourself with the raising of these two fine cubs."

She lifted then her small three-cornered hat from her hair and tossed the dark, loose locks. She glanced at the circle of string in her hands and with a graceful gesture she lifted it and put it round her neck. Then she put her hat back on and went to the oval Chippendale mirror by the doorway and admired the thing on her throat.

"I may end up in a stouter string than this," she laughed.

"But, at least, I can say I had this one from the hands of friends."

Sally, still in her nightdress, stayed behind indoors as I followed Barbara out into the snow and watched as Wherry handed her the bridle of her black horse.

"Barbary?"

"What, Dan?"

"Why would you fear to stay and marry Major Henthorn?"

"Why, then I might come to love him," she answered.

"Why not?" asked I, who knew little of love in those green years.

"Never mind, cub," she said. "It all wants too much explaining."

I was glad Sally was not there to see because then Barbara bent again and kissed me.

"Just let it rest at this," she said, softly. "That once I knew your father, Daniel Cresap."

And with that she was off and away down the river road in the snow.

Sally and I stayed on at Major Henthorn's house.

The day did not pass in which Sally's marvelling new eyes did not discover some fresh wonder in the world of our river kingdom. And the more Sally saw, the more I saw in Sally, as if my own eyes, too, had long been strangely blind.

ABOUT THE AUTHOR

DAVIS GRUBB was born in Moundsville, West Virginia, a small town on the Ohio River where one of the largest remaining prehistoric mound formations is located. His family had lived in the area for over two hundred years, so from early childhood he was well acquainted with the river lore and the legendary rogues and rascals of the region, all of which played a large part in shaping his literary imagination.

He worked his way through one year in art school at the Carnegie School of Technology by sorting stuffed Guatemalan hummingbirds in the ornithology department, but abandoned his studies because of color blindness. This was not a disappointment since he had chosen literature as a career at the age of seven.

He is the author of *The Night of the Hunter, A Dream of Kings,* and *The Voices of Glory.* Mr. Grubb lives in New York City, is forty-nine and single. His roommate is a Lhasa Apso named Rowdy Charlie.